The Dream Stealer

The Dream Stealer

Gregory Maguire

HARPER & ROW, PUBLISHERS

Library of Congress Cataloging in Publication Data
Maguire, Gregory.
   The dream stealer.

   Summary: A village of Russian peasants rebuild their
homes on a train to flee an evil wolf, only to be saved
by a little girl's dream and the knowledge of the witch
Baba Yaga.
   [1. Wolves—Fiction.   2. Soviet Union—Fiction
3. Fantasy]   I. Title.
PZ7.M2762Dr 1983   [Fic]   82-48854
ISBN 0-06-024031-8
ISBN 0-06-024032-6 (lib. bdg.)

Designed by Al Cetta
1 2 3 4 5 6 7 8 9 10
First Edition

HERE'S A BOOK FOR MY NEPHEWS AND NIECES (SO FAR):

DANIEL AND JUSTIN MAGUIRE

STEPHEN AND PETER AND ANNE-MARIE MACDONELL

MATTHEW AND ROBERT MAGUIRE—

WITH LOVE COMING AT THEM LIKE A TIDAL WAVE

FROM THEIR UNCLE GREG

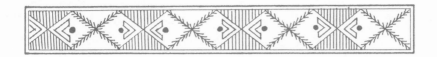

Contents

The Dream Stealer

Rumors and Omens

"Who told you that? Such rubbish! Do you believe everything you hear? You're not nine years old anymore, Pasha, you're ten: Ten is old enough to stop believing such nonsense."

At a table, two people: Pasha and his grandfather Ivan. Pasha was far too young to have a beard. Ivan was so old his beard brushed the edge of the table and picked up crumbs from the brown bread they were eating. Well, Ivan was eating it. Pasha was just sitting.

"Was it Old Sophia, the gossip hag, telling you such things?"

Pasha didn't answer. (Old Sophia was the culprit, however, telling Pasha of all these dangers.)

Ivan had been born with two sets of eyebrows, and all through his life he'd been able to scowl at the world with twice the ferocity of other people. When he looked across the table at Pasha and announced that there was *no such wolf* as the Blood Prince, Pasha shivered and believed him wholeheartedly.

But when his grandfather left the room, gone out

1

to confer with the other old men of the village of Miersk, Pasha felt less sure, and the name of the worst wolf in the world came nudging up at his imagination, nibbling at his thoughts, saying itself over and over again in Pasha's mind: *Blood Prince, Blood Prince. Blood Prince.*

Once, in return for his having carried a bundle of sticks to her hut, Old Sophia let him look at the triangular bit of reflecting glass she had found by the side of the road. Pasha couldn't see his whole face; the mirror was too small. But he found one eye, and then after moving a little he found the other one too. Above each eye was one ordinary wheat-colored eyebrow. If he'd had two eyebrows for each eye as his grandfather did, maybe he could have expected to be like his grandfather in other ways, too: fearless of the Blood Prince, a thunderstorm against any little worry. But God had anointed him with only a normal supply of eyebrows. No more, no less.

"You look at yourself as a girl would," jeered Old Sophia, pushing him away from the glass, forcing a bit of sausage into his hands. "Go on, eat up and get yourself manly. You're a good soul, Pasha, but the moon's in your eyes. You've got to be strong if you're going to survive the Blood Prince."

But surely no one really believes in the Blood Prince, not in these modern times, thought Pasha as he trudged home through melting snow and bristling bracken, along the edge of the railroad tracks.

❧❧❧

So suppose you've just arrived in Miersk, and suppose someone has set out to show you the village—say Old

Sophia, the gray-headed authority on village gossip. Old Sophia will start out your tour at the edge of the railroad tracks, because the railroad is the only way to get to Miersk at all—the only sensible way. If you've come through the woods you are either mad or foolish or you long to meet your maker. If it's a wolf year, you won't have made it through the woods on foot.

Or if you've escaped the wolves, then you've been saved for the hungry iron teeth of Baba Yaga. Which is far worse.

"Away to the south," says Old Sophia, "past Bovgorod, if you follow the tracks, you get to Moscow. They say Moscow is like a dozen villages braided together into one big one. I don't know, for I've never been. Away to the north are the lakes and fields and forests, and the vacation homes of the gentry: the rich towns of Plimst and Vlidir. And all the travelers ride the Imperial Express through the humble ragtag village of Miersk."

You look around. You don't see much: a rich doughy dark mud into which a handful of ramshackle log huts are tilting and sinking. A chapel with a bright-blue onion-dome spire, the only well-kept building in town. If you look for streets, you don't find any, just paths worn down to dirt, passages where people rush through the snow or the lemony-yellow grasses, depending on the season.

You turn away and look on the other side of the tracks to see if perhaps the village of Miersk is really over there, and if this is just a poor adjacent neighborhood.

3

"No, this is it," says Old Sophia sadly, seeing your face. "Not much to say about it. Here it is."

"Old Sophia, my mother says you're to come eat a meal with us," calls Pasha, running through the muddy ruts. "Beets and onions tonight for supper!"

Old Sophia excuses herself and hobbles away, her hands in her apron, leaving you alone at the edge of the tracks.

But you're not there, not really, you just would never come. Nobody ever gets off the Imperial Express to have a look at Miersk. Nobody wants to.

Some years there was a teacher, and some years there wasn't. If there was a teacher, Pasha took his lessons in the station house; if there wasn't a teacher, Pasha ran about and never noticed the lack of lessons.

When Pasha was smaller, gone to the first afternoon of his first lessons, the bearded teacher had said, "And now who is the family that you spring from, little salt head?"

Pasha had said, "First is my grandfather Ivan, one of the elders of Miersk. He has two eyebrows over each eye and he is the one who persuaded the railway men to build the tracks through Miersk. Way long ago, before there was a train here. Then is my father, Peter, and my mother, Onya.

"Then is me, Pasha. And then is the cow, Milkface, and the chickens, Cluck and Clack—we have only two names for the chickens even though sometimes there are more chickens than two—and the cat, Mousetrap. And we never give names to the mice, because they

4

are always dead when we get to them. Mousetrap does a good job with her claws."

The teacher loomed over Pasha. His beard seemed to grow extra inches in astonishment. "The beasts of the barn are your family?"

"We don't have a barn," said Pasha, confused, knowing he was saying things the teacher didn't want to hear. "Just a shed with two walls and a sort of roof."

"And the stars are your cousins, I suppose? And snails?" said the teacher.

Pasha didn't know about that. He didn't say anything.

"And the moon's your uncle, and the sun is your grandfather," said the teacher. "How about spiders?"

"I'm not related to any spiders," said Pasha, "not as far as I know, anyway."

The teacher smiled. "A boy whose relatives are the creatures of the world. Well, may they never all come to dine on the same night, little salt head."

It was Pasha's job to bring Milkface home from the field at sunset every day. He forgot every day until the light got thick and bronzed and dusty, and the sun sank brightly behind smoke-black trees, and then he ran to the field, sorted Milkface out from the other cows, and led her home. She wore a rich scent of mud and munchings, and she seemed to hover behind Pasha on the path like a big dark cloud with a bone-white face.

Sometimes the Imperial Express would race past, its wheels spinning out a musical drumlike sound from the shining rails, its passengers elegant and doll-like behind the maroon drapes at the windows. Milkface

5

would raise her blessed head and moo a greeting. Pasha often wondered if she thought the Imperial Express was a sort of angel cow who moved like wind, bellowing out a companionable blast as it steamed by. He would put his arms around Milkface's neck, as far as they would reach, so she wouldn't feel lonely being left behind.

Pasha wasn't even scared of wolves when he was with Milkface. If a pack were to come skulking forward out of the brush, he knew he would leap up on Milkface, and one by one Milkface would calmly kick their brains out as they approached. She had no patience with pests, and she was very loyal.

Of course, Pasha always knew that the Blood Prince would be the end of gentle Milkface. If there was such a demon wolf.

❧❧❧❧❧

"It's a story of old wives and little children," said Ivan after the meal of beets and onions and hunks of dark bread. "Whoever believes in such an impossible beast is a fool."

"May I be a fool and live a good long foolish life," said Old Sophia, glaring at Ivan. "Amen."

Pasha picked up Mousetrap and put his face next to her whiskers.

"Still," said Peter, "still, old father, the rumors are flying again. Leo Maryushka, the train conductor, said that the servants in the grand houses of Plimst and Vlidir are deserting their posts. The noble families have no one to serve their meals or drive their carriages. He said that the noble families would be ending their summer stays earlier this year."

"So rumors have always flown. Name a single soul who has met the Blood Prince in person."

"There is no one—" said Peter.

"AHA!" said the old man, twitching all his eyebrows.

"—who has lived to tell about it," said Peter.

"Stop this talk, you're scaring the boy," said Quiet Onya. "I am going off to take some soup to Father Dimitri, and to walk Old Sophia to her hut. Pasha, would you check the pen? There is a fox abroad, and we don't want to lose Cluck or Clack, not till we're ready."

"Thank you for your food. For your proud opinions, no thanks at all," said Old Sophia to Ivan, and then she left with Quiet Onya.

"I can see that I'm not being taken seriously," said the old man. "I tell you, I've lived in the shadows of this dark forest more years than any of you can count. Stories about the Blood Prince crop up every score of years or so. All nonsense. Always was. As if we didn't have enough to worry about with the winters and the wolves and the moods of Baba Yaga, we have to invent stories about an imaginary wolf. Fear seems to be our favorite pastime."

Peter, to respect his father, held back from arguing; but he stood before the stove and then turned with his hands all warmed, and he made the Sign of the Cross over the room.

Even the old man didn't grumble at the Sign of the Cross.

But as Pasha scurried up the rough-hewn pegs to his blankets in the loft, he heard the old man mutter, "Well, anyone who really needs to know should ask

Baba Yaga. She'd tell you there was nothing to fear in the Blood Prince."

"Yes, and then she'd eat you herself," said Peter.

The old man didn't protest that.

⚬⚬⚬⚬⚬

Lisette was on the platform at the station. It was noon, and the train that had passed through the town yesterday going north would be coming through today, going south. The Imperial Express would be heard in the distance, hooting a proud warning. Above the tree line a charcoal tunnel of smoke would bore its way through the empty glassy air of sunlit noon, and then far down the tracks from around the curve the engine would emerge, its smokestack dragging the tunnel of smoke behind it, brilliant flashes of ember red sparkling in the black.

There were folk bolder than Lisette who dared to stand near the edge of the platform for a better spot to sell from—Old Sophia, when she was well, would stand so near the rails that her nose and chin were in danger of being flattened ("Not such a bad thing, for that old woman," muttered a jealous competitor one day). But Lisette, being a little girl, was scared that the force of the Imperial Express, even as it slowed down to stop at Miersk, would be great enough to pull her knees and skinny elbows and small frame head-first into the giant iron wheels, wheels as large around as tree trunks and braced with greasy iron spokes, wheels which would show no mercy and chew her up. So Lisette always hung toward the back of the crowd until the Imperial Express had come to a full stop.

By then the mechanics and the conductors were

8

leaping off the train to run for the water and fuel which the men of Miersk supplied—for a fee—and the passengers were throwing open the windows of their compartments, tossing down coins, reaching for bread and potatoes and whatever else the women of Miersk had to sell.

"Fine bread, buy here from a Christian child," Lisette cried, darting forward between Old Sophia and Quiet Onya. She smiled at the passengers, who pointed out what they wanted, anxious to stock up before the train began to move again. Lisette never sold as much as the veterans, Old Sophia, Quiet Onya, other spry women with their quick exchanges and long arms. But she brought home money for her father and her little brother, and there were pretty men and women on the train who gave her a little extra for her youth and shyness.

The train didn't stop for long. Passengers rarely disembarked, as they were headed for the towns of Plimst and Vlidir (on one end of the line) or Bovgorod and Moscow (on the other). And except for the traveling schoolteacher, no one in Miersk ever boarded; no one could afford to. When the train had gone again, leaving the platform foul with its stink, the women sat down to count coins and compare earnings. Lisette sat with them.

"Leo Maryushka is right," the women agreed among themselves. "Fewer gentlefolk going to Plimst and Vlidir. The awful stories of the wretched wolf are scaring the property owners away from their summer homes. We'll go hungrier this winter—the trade in bread and vegetables is terrible now."

9

One woman began to cry, turning up the edges of her shawl to catch her tears. "My husband wants to leave Miersk," she said, "before the wolf gets here. I go to Father Dimitri, and he tells me to obey my husband. But how can we leave our only home?"

"How can we afford to stay if we will be eaten?" said Quiet Onya. "Peter's old father says that only Baba Yaga can tell us if the rumor has the taste of truth to it. But who will go looking for her?"

No one spoke.

I will, said Lisette inside her own head. But she didn't say it aloud. She couldn't. She was just trying it out in her head to hear how it sounded to be brave.

⊱⊰⊱⊰⊱⊰

When there was time apart from chores and prayers, selling bread and tending the cow, Pasha and Lisette were friends.

"I'd rather be friends with a boy, but there aren't any boys my age in Miersk," admitted Pasha one day as they were balancing on the railroad tracks, walking away from the village.

"If you wait for eight years, then my brother Vanya will be your age—he'll be old enough to be your friend," said Lisette helpfully.

"That's a long wait," said Pasha.

They stopped to throw stones at a stream.

"Besides, then I will be eighteen," said Pasha. "I'll be an old man."

Lisette counted. "I'll be seventeen then," she said. "Nearly a grandmother."

"I wonder if we'll still know each other?" said Pasha.

"Who else would we know?" demanded Lisette.

10

"There's nobody else our age in the village except us."

"Well, anyway," said Pasha, "I'd rather have you be my friend than Vanya. He cries too much."

"That's his job. He's not even two years old yet," said Lisette.

"I like you better than I like him, anyway," said Pasha.

"I cry too," said Lisette, "only usually when no one can see me."

"I'm trying to tell you I'm glad we're friends!" yelled Pasha.

"I know you are! So am I! Don't yell at me!" yelled Lisette back at him.

There was a rustle in the bushes on the other side of the stream; something had been awakened by their shouting. "It's the fox that's been after our hens, stupid thing," said Pasha, peering. "I think it is. If my grandfather finds it, he'll kill it. Go off, fox!" He threw a stone into the undergrowth, to scare it away.

"Pasha, don't; what if it's the wolf—" began Lisette.

"It couldn't be, not in broad daylight . . ." and then Pasha was speechless.

Up from the brambles like a fountain of liquid copper sprayed the brilliant feathers and luminous wings of a Firebird. For an instant it hung in the air above them, bright as the icons in the holy corners of their huts. The stream was so dazzled by the apparition that it stopped flowing, and a reflection of the bird showed in the suddenly still water. Pasha and Lisette both realized later that the Firebird had been so bright that they had been mostly staring at the reflection in the water rather than at the bird itself.

And then, with a flapping of its wings sounding like a wind blowing deep at the bottom of the sea, the Firebird lifted into the air and flew away beyond the silver birches, back toward the village. Pasha and Lisette found themselves stumbling to the edge of the water, dipping their hands in, trying to stir the reflection back, blessing themselves.

Oh, you didn't want to hear the shouting that went on in Lisette's hut that night! It was as if Lisette's father had had too much vodka.

His name was Grishka, and he rolled bowls around the room in his fury, and Lisette had to carry small bawling Vanya in her arms to keep him from being hit. "You see a Firebird and you catch it," he yelled. "You pull out a feather from its tail, you know that! How could you be so stupid! You had a chance at capturing a magic Firebird!"

Lisette's mother didn't intervene for her daughter because she was dead and laid to rest.

"We could have taken the feather and brought it to the Tsar! You could have become a duchess! Carriages and money and servants in reward for the feather of a Firebird! How could you be so slow!" *Crash, crash.* Lisette's legs were busy leaping. Her father had a short temper, and she leapt away from Grishka's tirades regularly—but her legs were strong.

Maybe it was worse at Pasha's hut. Nobody believed him when he told them that he had flushed a Firebird out of the bushes where the railroad tracks crossed the stream.

"Pasha, my young one, there's only a hair's difference between being a storyteller and being a liar," said old Ivan. "Even tall people with whiskers and learning sometimes forget the difference. Mind your tongue— it can set loose a lot of very pretty lies."

"Oh, but I am telling the truth tonight," cried Pasha. "On the cross. I swear it!"

"And where's the feather of the Firebird? Surely you weren't dull enough to forget to try to catch it by the tail?"

"I did forget," said Pasha. "It was so beautiful."

"Show me the feather and I'll believe it," said Ivan. "Meanwhile, you should study your letters and learn to make them into words. When the teacher comes back you can write this story down."

"It's not a story, grandfather—I couldn't make up such a thing," said Pasha. "It was a bird made of stars and golden drops of water. I could never tell my head to think up such a bird."

Quiet Onya, sewing together strips of old cloth to make a new blanket for the winter, pursed her lips at Pasha; it was their private signal. It meant: Don't say anything more, it's not worth it. Pasha stared glumly at his mother and tried to imagine himself leaping to catch hold of the Firebird. He couldn't imagine it.

That night a fox caught poor Cluck and carried her away.

❧❧❧❧❧

Old Sophia was on her way to the station platform with her basket of bread and potatoes the next day when she spied Father Dimitri. She hated to interrupt the good man at his thoughts, but her appetite for gossip was huge. She greeted him with the proper

13

respect and then said, "Did you hear, Father, about the children of Grishka and Peter, and what they claim to have seen yesterday?"

"No," answered the priest, knowing full well Old Sophia would tell him.

"A Firebird, as sure as the sun shines," said the old woman, looking to the left and to the right. "Old Ivan with his eyebrows like mice just scowled at me when he told me, but those children aren't clever enough to make up a story like that."

"It's an omen," said the priest, stroking his beard.

"But what does it mean?" said Old Sophia. "And how could those children have forgotten to try to capture it? We all could have been pulled along to riches on the tailfeathers of a Firebird, the whole miserable little settlement of us."

"That the children didn't remember to grasp the tailfeathers of a Firebird is the omen," said Father Dimitri.

"But what does it mean?" Old Sophia peered into the face of the priest.

"I don't read omens," said the good man. "I pray for them to occur and leave the reading of them up to Baba Yaga." He cloaked his face in an expression of deep thought and hurried off to the chapel.

"But who will ask Baba Yaga?" called Old Sophia.

There was no answer. The old woman turned back toward the platform where the other women were gathered, awaiting the noon water stop of the Imperial Express, and she shared with them the question: Who will ask Baba Yaga what the omen means?

"I saw Baba Yaga once, when I was a little girl," said Old Sophia on the railroad platform. "I saw her from a distance, flying in her narrow wooden mortar; she stood in it like a doll waist deep in a vase. She was sweeping a flock of terrified geese before her with her broom. She drove the geese headfirst into a sheer cliffside, where they were killed and fell to the ground. What she did with the bodies I don't know. I didn't stay to see. I didn't have the nerve to converse with her then and I don't now either."

"Old Sophia, scared of Baba Yaga!" jeered the conductor, Leo Maryushka, leaping back onto the train. Old Sophia threw a potato at him. "Without my fear I'd be a simpleton," she called after him. To the women on the platform she said, "I consider that a potato well spent."

"Ah, old Baba Yaga," said a woman, spitting on the ground. "I've never seen her, and I hope I never will. She's a recluse; no one knows her well, and she knows no one well. I doubt she's ever even heard of Miersk. She lives in her hut—sometimes near us, they say, sometimes thousands of miles away. Who's to tell? I'd be scared to go looking for her myself."

"I can't forsake the chapel to go off looking for Baba Yaga," said Father Dimitri. "It could take weeks to find her. I can't leave the chapel untended for that long."

"And who's to say that she won't be in an ill humor when she's found?" suggested Grishka. "Gnash at

15

the poor wanderer and serve him up as a stew?"

"Bah," said old Ivan. "We want nothing to do with that Baba Yaga. What we need to know we can figure out for ourselves. And I still don't believe little Pasha ever saw a Firebird."

Quiet Onya said, "My son doesn't tell lies—he is a good boy."

Peter said, "He is a good boy, our Pasha. But every week the Imperial Express carries more passengers back to Moscow, and soon the traffic will be dried up for the year. The tales of the Blood Prince grow more and more vivid. If there is an omen in the coming of the Firebird, we must know what it is."

Pasha and Lisette met in the shadow of the chapel.

"Everyone is saying that someone should ask Baba Yaga why we forgot to steal a feather from the tail of the Firebird," said Pasha. "And my old sour grandfather still doesn't believe that we ever saw it. He's taken to calling me Pasha the Liar."

"If we went and asked her," said Lisette, "they'd believe you then. Baba Yaga doesn't lie."

"Are you brave enough to go?" said Pasha.

"No," said Lisette, "but I'll try. When my mother died, she said, 'Lisette, everything flowers eventually. Be brave while you're waiting.' So I should at least try to be brave."

The next night, they decided, they'd hunt for Baba Yaga.

"Does she really have iron teeth?" asked Lisette.

"So they say," said Pasha.

"Rusty breath," said Lisette.

"Sharp bite," said Pasha.

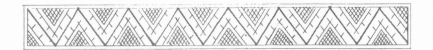

The Search for Baba Yaga

It was a bad day.

Ivan was elaborately ignoring Pasha until he admitted that there had been no Firebird. If Pasha had had any hesitation about leaving to hunt for Baba Yaga, it was gone now. He couldn't wait to go.

Lisette kissed her baby brother Vanya over and over again, and then ran out to the station with tears in her eyes. Her mother had told her to be brave, but she didn't think she was doing very well.

The sky was full of stringy clouds that looked as if they wanted to rain. Everyone in the village was upset and nobody would admit it out loud.

Leo Maryushka brought bad news for the women—and for all of them. "You'd better start making pancakes out of those potatoes," he told them. "We're cutting down the run from Plimst and Vlidir from three times a week to two. And maybe it'll go lower."

"Oh, we are surely a luckless lot," said Old Sophia, speaking for them all. "The wolf on the prowl and the hunger in the gut. How are we going to survive?"

"You're a smart lot, you people of Miersk," said Leo Maryushka. "And where your smartness leaves off, your stubbornness takes over. You'll get by."

The trading that afternoon was halfhearted. Leo Maryushka bought some bread from Lisette, though everyone knew he always carried a lunch of cheese and beer with him. When the Imperial Express had steamed away, sending its plume of inky smoke to the lowering clouds, the women sat on the steps of the platform and didn't even bother to count their earnings.

"It's an ugly little place, Miersk," said one woman after a long pause. "I'd go to Saint Petersburg in an instant if I could."

"It's all we've got, mud and muck and houses leaning over onto each other," said another woman with a cold sort of passion in her voice, "and it doesn't treat us very well, but it's my home and I could never leave it."

"Where did the rumors of the Blood Prince start?" asked a third woman.

Quiet Onya spoke up. "Old Ivan says that stories about the Blood Prince come from our own weakhearted fear of everything. That if it wasn't the Blood Prince, it would be something else. That it's all a fear without a foundation in truth."

"Do you believe him, eh, Quiet Onya?" asked Old Sophia.

"He's my husband's father—what am I supposed to do?" said Quiet Onya. She tugged at her babushka to make it cover more of her forehead, and leaned forward and said distinctly, "No."

"Why not?" asked Lisette, in a voice that walked back and forth between two notes, unsure of which one it wanted to depend on.

Quiet Onya made the Sign of the Cross and said, "My own mother, may she rest in peace, used to tell me about the time she was surrounded in a forest by a dozen unfriendly bears. They came, drawn by her campfire, to see who was there and to eat up whoever it was. My mother said her hair stood straight up off her head in fright and it made her nine feet tall. But the bears were not impressed and continued to close in. Where is my husband? she screamed. Why doesn't he come back from collecting firewood? And then do you know what happened?"

"She got eaten?" said Lisette.

"No. She heard, not far away, the awful cry of a wolf. And she was so frightened that the wolf was eating her husband that she picked up a stick out of the fire and chased the bears away with its flaming end held up high."

"Did her husband get eaten?" asked Lisette.

"No. He was very close by. He was gathering firewood as calm as you please. He never heard the cry of the wolf or my mother's scream. He told my mother she imagined it, and so she told me: Onya, don't be a fool. Believe in your imaginings, frightening as they are. They may give you the courage to fight a dozen bears."

That's the courage I need to face Baba Yaga with, thought Lisette.

"And even besides that, I think the Blood Prince is real," said Quiet Onya. "I just do."

At the edge of the meadow Pasha stood and looked at the cows. They were gathered near the stream, their heads down to the grass, their tails swishing at flies. Pasha tried to see them clearly, but his eyes were troubled with tears, and he couldn't pick Milkface out from the lot. "Milkface, come home," he said, but he knew his voice was weak and wouldn't carry.

There had been bad times before in Miersk. Everyone talked about them all the time. The terrible fire! The yellowing fever! The time that there was no rain for two years! But this bad time seemed realer because it was happening *now*, and Pasha was *in* it. The Blood Prince might be on the prowl—or he might not, if he was just a rumor. But rumor or not, the fear of him was drying up the train traffic, and they depended on the train for their income. No money, no food. A bad, bad time.

Pasha was crying in case he never saw Milkface again. In case he and Lisette got lost in the forest and starved to death, or got caught by bears and eaten alive, or displeased Baba Yaga when they finally found her and got starved to death and eaten alive at the same time.

If Pasha never came back, Milkface would go on munching and swishing and plodding along, and she would never really miss Pasha. Just in the back of her cow mind there might be a little stir of memory, a little affectionate trembling every now and then for some small human creature who had been kind to her.

"Oh, Milkface," cried Pasha, sitting in the ferns,

"what if I don't come back? What will happen to everything?"

But Milkface wasn't a very smart cow. In fact, she'd never even learned her own name. So Pasha kept wiping the tears from his eyes and the cows kept tasting the greens, and the sun began to think about being tired and going home.

∂≈∂≈∂≈∂

It would be easier to leave if they didn't look back, they decided. So as the night began to spread its dark shadows along the edges of the small houses of Miersk, Pasha and Lisette met at the edge of the train tracks and began walking north. They kept their promise; they didn't look back.

"Maybe we should have left a note," said Lisette when they'd been walking about two minutes.

"My parents don't read," Pasha reminded her, "nor does your father."

They passed the place where they'd seen the Firebird. Now that place was just a regular damp tangled bit of stream edge.

"My mother says that Baba Yaga puts the skulls of her enemies on poles," said Pasha, "and that their eyes shine with yellow light."

"I've heard that too," said Lisette. "Does it always get this dark at night?"

"I think so," said Pasha.

The train tracks made an easy path to follow. The iron rails reflected what little light there was, from stars and comets; the rails stretched out like four endless moonbeams nailed down to the earth. For a while the trip was even fun.

21

"Maybe we should have told somebody where we were going," said Lisette.

"They'll know," said Pasha. "All that talk about Baba Yaga? They'll know."

"They say Baba Yaga lives in a hut that stands on two chicken legs in a clearing," said Lisette.

"Do you want to hold my hand?" asked Pasha.

"Is it true about the hut with chicken legs?"

"Yes."

Lisette reached out and took Pasha's hand.

After a while Pasha said, "You know, Lisette, it's not likely that Baba Yaga's hut is going to be standing right in the middle of the train tracks. We're going to have to go looking in the woods sooner or later."

"Later," said Lisette.

"I mean, after all," said Pasha, "think of what would happen to the poor train if it crashed into Baba Yaga's hut. The old witch would turn the entire train into a snake and swallow it whole."

"I have an idea," said Lisette. "Let's not talk about Baba Yaga."

"What do you want to talk about?" said Pasha politely.

Lisette couldn't think of anything, so she sang a song. It went like this:

> *"When I dream, I dream of you.*
> *Does that make you dream of me?*
> *Dreamers holding hands are we,*
> *Dreaming things that soon will be."*

"That's a nice song," said Pasha.

"My mother taught it to me," said Lisette.

"I wouldn't sing it too loudly right now, in case Baba Yaga is near," said Pasha. "She might think you were dreaming of holding hands with *her*."

They didn't sing or talk anymore. After a while they crawled in under a bush by the side of the railroad tracks and went to sleep. Both of them dreamed of each other.

When they awoke the next morning and realized that they hadn't been eaten by bears or wolves during the night, they were quite pleased. Pasha found a little stream not far from the tracks, and they both washed in it. Lisette unrolled a small loaf from the scarf she'd been carrying tied to her apron strings, and they ate bread and drank water and tried to finger the knots out of each other's hair.

"It's a bright day," said Lisette, "so clean and clear that even Baba Yaga might not be so bad to see. A good day for finding her."

"She probably hates days like today," said Pasha. "She probably drapes a black shawl over her face to keep the sun out."

Lisette couldn't be daunted. She sang her mother's song again and made up a game out of walking on the rails, a hopping, humming, irritating sort of game. Pasha felt annoyed and didn't speak much.

"Look, Lisette, sooner or later we're going to have to leave the tracks," he said. "We've been walking an hour, and maybe the Imperial Express will fly along the tracks and crush us. It's not smart."

"Well, which way will the train be coming?" asked Lisette. "If it's heading north, we just walk on the southbound tracks. Or the other way around."

"Yesterday's train came from the south, so we should be on the northbound tracks, not the southbound," said Pasha.

"Well, which is which?" asked Lisette.

They both looked at the parallel sets of tracks, and they couldn't think of which was which.

"We'll hear it coming, I guess," Pasha finally decided, "as long as you don't hum too loudly."

"I don't hum louder than a *train*," said Lisette, hurt.

So they walked along without speaking for a while, until they rounded a gradual curve and found themselves staring at the slope-floored platform of the humble train station of the village of Miersk.

"What did we do?" whispered Pasha in disbelief.

"We got turned around in our sleep," said Lisette. "We've gone backward. Maybe it was the magic of Baba Yaga."

"We can't go home yet. It's too soon," said Pasha.

"Maybe we can just peek in and see how everyone is," said Lisette. "I wonder if Papa remembered to feed Vanya his breakfast."

"We can't go that close," said Pasha, "but maybe we can hide under the train-station floor and hear what people say about our being missing."

"I want to see little Vanya," protested Lisette, but Pasha wouldn't allow it. So they hid in the dusty shadows under the train station, and after a while they heard footsteps crossing the boards above them.

※※※※※

"Hello, old crone," said a familiar voice—it was Ivan with the four eyebrows.

"Hello, old sourbeard," said another familiar voice—Old Sophia. "You're not off praying with Father Dimitri about the safe return of the little runaways?"

"The good Father has enough experience in praying without needing the help of an amateur," said the voice of Ivan. "I've come down to speak with the conductor when the train makes its stop."

"What can Leo Maryushka do for you?" said the voice of Old Sophia.

"I'll ask him to keep a lookout for the children. More likely than not, they followed the train tracks away from the village. Maybe he'll see a campfire, or maybe he'll even see *them*. Pick them up, bring them home."

"How is Quiet Onya bearing up under Pasha's disappearance?"

"Oh, she wails and tears at her hair. What do you expect; she's his mother. She'll be all right."

"Maybe," whispered Pasha to Lisette, "we should just peek in a minute."

"*No,*" whispered Lisette. "You wouldn't let me, so you can't either. Shhh."

"They're not out looking for the children? Quiet Onya and Peter?" The voice of Old Sophia sounded surprised.

"There are endless spreads of forest on either side of Miersk," said the voice of Ivan. "One by one we could go out searching and one by one be lost forever. I have forbidden Quiet Onya and Peter to wander off to look for the children. The little ones will come back by themselves, contrite and ashamed and deserving of a fierce beating."

"You are a heartless man, Ivan. Suppose the children actually do find Baba Yaga? Assuming that was their goal?"

"There's no telling the moods of old Baba Yaga," said the voice of Ivan. "Sometimes she boils little children into soup and sometimes she turns around and gives them a bit of magic that makes everything right. I don't trust her for a minute. But I do know one thing."

"Oh, you know a thing. Surprise," said the voice of Old Sophia. "Delight me with it."

"Don't be funny, old woman. How well Baba Yaga reacts to the children depends on one thing."

"And that is—?"

"Whether or not she has already seen the Firebird. If *she* has not seen it and the children tell her that *they* have, she may be so furious at being bettered that she will kill them on the spot. But if she *has* seen it and the children ask her about it, she may be flattered and answer their question graciously, and send them safely home."

"I—"

"You know how changeable that old witch is. Remember the story of Vasilissa the Beautiful? Baba Yaga befriended her and gave her the magic doll for help. And yet there are stories about her being fierce and wicked as well."

"You—"

"Who's to tell what sort of charm—a magic doll, a spell, a good luck piece—she might give the children if she has already seen the Firebird herself, and feels authoritative and knowing about it?"

"Now you believe in the Firebird. Do you also believe what everyone is saying, that if a magical Firebird appeared near Miersk, it's a warning from heaven that the Blood Prince is on his way? *Now? Here?* To *Miersk*, of all the flea-sized villages in Russia?"

"I'll believe in the Blood Prince when I see him."

"Hold your voice down and let me speak," said the voice of Old Sophia. "You speak now as if the Firebird really flew. But yesterday, and the days before that, you said that you didn't believe Pasha and Lisette had seen a Firebird. You said it so loudly that the whole village heard you. It was wicked of you to lie if you actually believed them all along."

"Who can believe Pasha?" asked the voice of the grandfather. "He has flower blossoms in his head instead of a brain. I didn't believe him until he and Lisette ran away. That convinced me."

"You are a hardhearted man, Ivan," said the voice of Old Sophia. "I would like to tie all your eyebrows into knots until you weep. It will be on your shoulders if those two innocent cubs are slaughtered by the old witch."

"You shouldn't talk to me like that," roared the voice of Ivan.

"I shouldn't talk to you at all, and hereafter I won't," replied the voice of Old Sophia.

◦◦◦◦◦

After the train had come, and the little commerce between villagers and passengers was concluded, Ivan spoke seriously to Leo Maryushka about the missing children, and then the train pulled away and the women counted their meager earnings and wandered off.

Then Pasha and Lisette set out, a second time, to find Baba Yaga.

The day was still brilliant, but the children's spirits were not so high. They were tired from their long journey of the previous day, and they were not happy about the chances of being boiled into soup.

"Maybe this was not a good idea," Lisette finally suggested. "Maybe someone else ought to have gone looking for Baba Yaga. Maybe we're too young."

"I don't like it any more than you do," said Pasha. They had left the tracks finally—having headed south from Miersk this time—and were pushing slowly through the thick undergrowth of a young forest. The sun was so excluded by the crowding leaves of the trees that the sky showed above them as only occasional jagged patches of distant faded blue. "But nobody else would go. Nobody believed me about the Firebird. So who would risk the visit to Baba Yaga?"

"But now your grandfather believes you," said Lisette. "Maybe we should have come out from under the railway platform and let *him* go."

"It's too late for that," said Pasha. "You should have had that idea earlier." And to himself he said, I don't want to see him for a while anyway. But it was too bad the old man wasn't racked with worry. It was too bad he wasn't a little bit hysterical with grief.

They crossed a stream. They went up knolls and down slopes. They parted, skirting big trees, and met again on the other side. Sometimes they didn't talk, sometimes they did.

"Does your father believe in the Blood Prince?" asked Pasha.

Lisette said, "He believes in everything, just in case it's true. He bows to Father Dimitri and then swears by the Devil, to keep friendly with all parties. He told me the Blood Prince was more than a rumor—it was a prophecy, a curse."

"What did your mother think before she died? Do you know?"

But Lisette only sang her mother's song again.

> *"When I dream, I dream of you.*
> *Does that make you dream of me?*
> *Dreamers holding hands are we,*
> *Dreaming things that soon will be."*

Two mornings later Pasha and Lisette woke early. Rain was tumbling down with the fury of spring waterfalls, pushing the summer undergrowth flat against the ground, splashing up gobs of mud, lacing the surface of the earth with a web of clear ropes of running water.

"Old Ivan is right," said Lisette. "We're going to go back to Miersk—and we'll have failed in our task. We can't go on in this deluge, Pasha. It's impossible to *move* in this forest. This is like being underwater."

"Courage," said Pasha. "Your mother reminded you to take heart."

"She never told me to learn how to swim," said Lisette. "My clothes are as wet as they get on washing day."

"We can't let old Ivan be right," said Pasha. "I couldn't stand it if he was."

"*Please*, Pasha," said Lisette, "can't we turn back? Old Ivan's temper won't kill you. It never has before."

"But this is a perfect day for walking in the woods," said Pasha. "All the dangerous beasts will stay in their dry caves and lairs. No Christian soul would be out on a day like today. We're perfectly safe."

"Beasts haven't got Christian souls," said Lisette, "and neither does Baba Yaga."

"Let's walk awhile. Maybe it'll let up."

So they splashed through the drenched forest, trampling down sodden ferns, leaning for breath against the trunks of dripping larches, squelching in pockets of mud. Pasha didn't speak because he didn't want Lisette to start pestering him to turn back. Lisette didn't speak because she was a little bit angry at Pasha. Their silence was balanced somewhere between them like a third person whom they didn't know very well, whose presence was keeping them from chattering to each other as they normally would have.

After a while the silence got mean, as if they were having a wordless fight. Who would speak first? Not me, not me, said Pasha inside himself. She wanted to come along, so she can just put up with a little rain. Lisette, inside *her*self, said: Oh, talk to me, look at me, even reach out to hold me steady as I try to jump across this stream. I *hate* walking silently in the middle of the woods, as if I were all alone, how *foolish*, how *childish*. I'd rather be with Vanya. At least he'd hold my hand even if he can't talk yet.

Finally Pasha said something. "Oh, look out, can't you?" Lisette had splashed him rather vigorously.

But not on purpose, Lisette said to herself, not sure

if that was true. She felt herself starting to cry and was glad of the rain: good disguise.

Then Pasha stopped and Lisette bumped into him and they both fell over into a thicket of seedling trees, and when Pasha reached out his hand to grab Lisette's she knew something was wrong, and she wiped her eyes as clear as they would get and looked ahead.

Baba Yaga.

The Train Is Late

Everyone expected Quiet Onya to be upset about her son's disappearance. It was only natural. Every day when their chores had been finished and the bread set to rise, the women of the town covered their heads with their outdoor shawls and hurried to the hut of Quiet Onya and Peter. With their striped skirts rustling and their crosses bouncing against their blouses, Old Sophia, Tanya, Olga, Marla, Bara, and Sweet Amelya came to listen to Quiet Onya wail out her worry. Sometimes they wailed along. Peter and old Ivan never stayed for long at the wailings.

But when Pasha and Lisette had been gone for *three full days*, the company of Tanya, Old Sophia, Olga, Marla, Bara, and Sweet Amelya braved the wet weather, expecting a rowdy afternoon of weeping and praying, only to find Quiet Onya sitting in a rickety chair in front of the fireplace, face as pale as lard, and very very quiet.

"Quiet Onya has become quiet again, what's this?" they murmured among themselves, somewhat disappointed; they'd come all prepared for a good loud cry.

Old Sophia pushed forward. "Quiet Onya, what is the meaning of this? Where is your *heart?*"

"My heart has turned to coal and crumbled," said Quiet Onya. "It has burned so hard that nothing is left but ashes."

"Have they found—a sock, a belt, a clue?" asked Old Sophia delicately. She was careful not to come right out and ask if they'd found Pasha's body.

"Not a clue," said Quiet Onya. She sat still for quite a while.

"Have you lost hope?" asked Tanya.

Quiet Onya just shrugged.

"I think she's lost hope," said Tanya to the others. "That's it, I'm sure. When I asked her if she'd lost hope, she merely shrugged. To me this means—"

"Shh," said Old Sophia. She looked around the room. "You haven't a loaf to rise today, Quiet Onya?"

"Why should I? For whom?" said Quiet Onya in a dry whisper.

"Why, for Ivan, of course, and your husband Peter, and for your little Pasha should he come back."

"I couldn't bear it!" cried Quiet Onya suddenly. "Old Ivan has forbidden me to leave the village to search for Pasha, but knowing that he might be wandering about cold, hungry, hurt—and with no one looking out for him . . ."

Old Sophia knelt down on the floor in front of Quiet Onya, and she spoke to her directly. "You go tell Leo Maryushka that when he next arrives in Bovgorod, he should alert the Tsar's men who patrol these forests that your Pasha is lost inside them. The Tsar's men will keep looking for him. There will always be a pair of eyes watching that way."

Quiet Onya nodded gratefully, and without a word she grabbed up her shawl and hurried out of her hut, on her way to the railroad station.

Tanya looked at Old Sophia in some puzzlement. "You know as well as I do that the Tsar's men never come near these parts. They're as scared of wolves, real or imagined, as we are. Your suggestion isn't going to help Pasha at all. And even if they did patrol the forests, do you think they'd pay attention to a missing peasant boy? They'd laugh at any suggestion of such nonsense!"

Old Sophia said, "My suggestion wasn't meant to help Pasha, but Quiet Onya instead. Give her some peace of mind. If she believes there is someone looking out for Pasha, it will provide her a little hope."

"Oh," said Tanya. "Well, you know best, Old Sophia."

"I don't know best at all," snapped Old Sophia, "but when I see Quiet Onya, who could find it in her heart to bake bread for every opening mouth in the Russias—when I see her sitting here with no loaf set out to rise—I know her heart is as ailing as if she'd been attacked by the Blood Prince herself!"

"Don't be agitated, Old Sophia. I believe you did the right thing," said Tanya humbly.

"Oh, we are surely a luckless lot," said Old Sophia grimly, and the women turned up their apron hems to their eyes and began their afternoon's wailing.

Grishka and Peter met Leo Maryushka on the platform when the Imperial Express came through Miersk. "Any sign of Pasha?" asked Peter; Grishka pushed him aside impatiently and said, "Lisette, my little turtledove, have you seen her?"

Leo Maryushka ran the length of the platform, his black boots making clopping sounds on the planks. He threw open the windows of the passenger coaches so that the few riders could buy their lunches. "No, no," he called behind him, his news as dampening as the weather, "not a word, not a sound, a hair. Nothing on the line but mist and water."

"It's the little boy, it's Vanya that gets to me," said Grishka to Peter as they loaded timber onto the train. "He is too small to understand where Lisette has gone. He cries all the time."

"You should bring him to see Quiet Onya and the others, he'd fit right in," said Peter darkly.

Leo Maryushka came near, snapping the windows back into place, sweating in the rain. "Things are so bad, the north line is so stirred up by the rumors of the Blood Prince, we may soon be closing down completely," he told them, "or at least until next spring. There are people migrating for the big cities every day; they want to leave before the snows come. The Blood Prince could wipe out a snowbound village in one night. The woods are filled with fleeing villagers. Someone will find the children and take care of them. You'll see. Exercise your faith in the goodness of things!"

35

But Quiet Onya pushed up to Leo before he could leap aboard again, and she begged him to listen to her for a minute. Bovgorod, she said, the Tsar's forest patrol, Pasha and Lisette, please would he respond to her sorrow and ask for their help—? Leo looked at Quiet Onya and said that he would, though as he turned and swung himself up onto the train he was thinking to himself that it was a hopeless request. . . .

Still, he had just admonished Grishka and Peter to exercise their faith in the goodness of things; so should he; he would fulfill his promise to Quiet Onya; he would go to the Tsar's men.

Pasha pinched himself and thought: I'm still alive. I've been in the presence of Baba Yaga for ten minutes and I'm still alive. Maybe it will be all right.

Lisette said to herself: Are we prisoners or guests of Baba Yaga? Perhaps she doesn't know the difference between taking prisoners and entertaining guests.

They walked in this order: Lisette, stumbling in the dripping shrubbery, obeying the bellowed instructions of Baba Yaga; then Pasha, who tried to keep branches from snapping back in the face of the witch (and thus preserve his life a bit longer); then Baba Yaga, standing upright in her flying mortar, poling her way through the woods with an oversized pestle.

Who knows what the old witch was thinking about when she came upon the two of them in the rain? No one ever knows what witches really think. And Baba Yaga was not a common witch.

As if it were frozen in his mind's eye and he would

never be able to imagine anything else, Pasha kept seeing Baba Yaga as she had first appeared.

Her face had been in the sky above them and her profile, facing left, made a jagged line against the moth-gray clouds. She never turned her face from that angle, but the one eye that had first spotted them—her left eye—fixed them with a stare like a lance. Her shawls and skirts (though no one with an ounce of sense would have dared criticize them) were filled with burns and burrs and awkward stitching—one big tear in her blouse had been woven together with the tail of a rat. The clothes were large and loose and dark and tended to swim away from Baba Yaga as if reluctant to come into actual contact.

The rat's tail kept twitching, though who knows how long ago it had been parted from its owner.

And while it had been a smart thought of Pasha's that no predators would leave their warm caves and dry lairs on such a wet summer's day as this, it hadn't applied to Baba Yaga. Rainwater never came near her. It parted above her head somewhere and fell in a circle a foot out from every side of her mortar. She was as dry as an old extracted tooth.

"So the mewling bits come poking through my forests, so they get a chance to poke through the door of my home as well!" she had said to them, and that was all she had said so far. Her voice was not what one would call musical.

My eyes are water, thought Lisette, my hair is water, this rain has made my clothes three times heavier than they ought to be. My stomach is water and I can hear water sloshing about in my knees and ankles. I will never beg to have a bath again. If I die in Baba Yaga's house there'll be no body to bury; I'll just go running and dripping right through the cracks in the floor.

But just when it seemed she couldn't bear it anymore, she saw a light between the larch trees up ahead.

And then they saw it.

Baba Yaga's house!

Exactly as described: a row of stakes encircling a clearing, stakes which were topped with grinning shiny-eyed skulls. And the house stood on two chicken legs in the center—but the chicken legs didn't stand still; they pawed the dirt and rushed about, and the house was carried about on top of them.

"So you dance about like a dumb child, so you get a knock in the face," shouted Baba Yaga, pushing up to the house and hitting the front door with her pestle.

The house seemed to come to its senses. It straightened up and stood still. Baba Yaga's mortar settled in the yard, and the witch climbed out and walked up to the house.

"Little house, let me come in," said Baba Yaga in a somewhat nicer voice.

The house bowed its front door down and Baba Yaga walked in. She called over her shoulder to the two luckless travelers, "Wait till I have the fire lit and the pot to boil."

In the yard, Lisette whispered, "Maybe this wasn't such a good idea, Pasha."

"We're here now," he whispered back. "Might as

well be calm about it. Might as well do what we came here for."

"You don't look calm," said Lisette, "at all. Your face is as white as a cooked egg."

"It all depends on if Baba Yaga has seen the Firebird herself or not," said Pasha. "That's what old Ivan says. If she has, we're in luck. If not—"

"Oh, what does your grandfather know about it?" said Lisette.

"He's Ivan. He has two sets of eyebrows," said Pasha.

"I know that. I'm not very impressed."

A voice rang out in the clearing, a new voice. "Baba Yaga, the two little people are talking all about you." It was one of the skulls, spying on them.

The old witch appeared at the door to her house. She looked with some interest at Pasha and Lisette squatting in the mud.

"I think it's time," said Baba Yaga. "Little house, put down your door and let them come in."

The women of Miersk had finally persuaded Quiet Onya that she had to continue her daily routine, or else she might just shrivel up and become dessicated with grief. On the morning when the sun finally showed itself again, Quiet Onya joined Old Sophia and the others at the railway platform, to greet the southbound Imperial Express at its noon stop.

"You're not the only one in grief, Quiet Onya," said one of the women. "My own sons set out for Bovgorod yesterday. They wanted to take me with them, but how could I leave the village of Miersk? It has been my only home."

Other women chimed in. The Blood Prince was a reality, the Blood Prince was a rumor. They should all leave Miersk, they should all stay. They would starve this winter without the rubles from the train trade, they would be eaten by the legendary wolf. They rubbed their arms and legs to keep warm, because although it was just the end of summer, a chill was beginning to spice the air.

Father Dimitri is saying special prayers against the wolf, someone said.

Grishka has taken to being gentle with his little Vanya, someone else said. Lisette's absence has softened him.

Well, it's a hard life he's had. A wife so lovely we called her Vasilissa the Beautiful, dying like that and leaving him with the two little ones, someone else said. No wonder he's been bitter as a lemon. He used to be kind and oh, handsome.

Old Sophia told them that her little triangular bit of mirror had become cloudy with all the recent rain. Maybe it's another omen, she said glumly.

Quiet Onya didn't say anything.

And until midafternoon they waited for the Imperial Express, Grishka and Peter and some of the other men throwing dice on the other end of the station platform, waiting to load the train up with water and coal, waiting to have a word with dashing Leo Maryushka, hoping the conductor had seen some clue of the missing children.

But the morning train didn't come, so everyone finally went home.

What was this?

If Baba Yaga was a gruesome witch, and if her skirts and shawls were black with the dirt of unspeakable crimes, and if the air around her smelled like the rotting of small animal bodies, and if her nervous house was surrounded by spying skulls with eerily lit eyes, and if she had the pot on to boil, perhaps to make soup out of her two visitors—if everything about this fearsome woman was rank and dark, then why did one corner of her hut shine as if a curving hair from the scalp of the blazing sun itself were hanging from a hook in the rafters?

After fifteen minutes in Baba Yaga's hut their eyes had adjusted to the gloom on one side and the radiant light on the other, and they could see Baba Yaga spinning about the room, throwing a pinch of this in the pot, and a pound of that, blossom of this weed and whisker of rat, stirring the obscure soup with the wing of a bat.

Neither Pasha nor Lisette was especially hungry.

They looked at each other with some concern, and whispered about what they would do. Neither of them felt brave enough to ask Baba Yaga about the omen, so they pulled a straw apart, and Pasha got the shorter piece. He waited till Baba Yaga had sunk, exhausted, into a heap of catskins and dead moths, and then he cleared his throat, and said in his best Russian politeness, "Old mother, may I ask you a question?"

"So you ask a question, so you suffer the consequences of the answer," murmured Baba Yaga, almost asleep.

Fair enough. Pasha said, "The question is about the Blood Prince, whether or not it exists. Have you heard that the Blood Prince is on the prowl?"

Baba Yaga opened one eyelid. Her eye seemed a yellow ember from the fires of hell. Baba Yaga and the Blood Prince are probably mother and son, Pasha thought wildly, expecting any second to die. He held Lisette's hand so tightly that the sweat couldn't even trickle between their fingers.

"If that's not a question you want to answer," said Pasha shakily, "there's another one. It's about the reading of an omen. Or something that might be an omen. I don't know for sure."

Baba Yaga opened the other eye, blue as the northern snow. (Her eyes could change color, Pasha noticed. Strange!)

"Go on till your doom, then stop," she ordered.

"It was a Firebird," said Pasha unhappily. "We flushed a Firebird out of the bushes near the railroad tracks running out of Miersk. We forgot to try to grab a feather. Is our forgetting an omen? What does it mean?"

Now or never: death or deliverance.

Baba Yaga whirled to her feet. "Your forgetting to grab a feather is no omen. You're just children yet, that's all, not greedy for power, ignorant of all that! No omen, just plain sense. But you tell me important things, and there is an omen to be read. Now. Now!"

She strode to the door of her hut, forgot to tell the house to lower its doorsill to the ground, fell eight feet, and kept walking. The children, glad to be still alive, followed at once, dropping with care out of the house—which obligingly leaned down low for *them*.

⸺❧❧❧⸻

Father Dimitri was coming from his evening devotions when he heard a long low tired sound, as if the forest itself were giving out a mighty breath. He blessed himself and thought: Even the forest finds these times trying.

He went and knocked on the door of the hut of Ivan and Peter and Quiet Onya. Ivan answered the knock, and Father Dimitri excused himself for interrupting, but did the men want to come outside and have a look around?

"What do you think it was?" said old Ivan, scowling with all his eyebrows. He wasn't overly fond of the priest; he found prayers something of a bother.

"It sounded to me," said Father Dimitri, running his hands through his beard, "as if the world were giving up. It was a sigh of capitulation. It was the last breath of hope."

Ivan looked so disgusted that the priest wondered fleetingly if perhaps *he* hadn't just breathed *his* last breath of hope. Ivan started in, "Your foolish talk—"

But his son, Peter, said, "Let's just have a look around now. No harm in that."

When they stood still they heard it, all of them: a labored string of sound, a smooth tired metallic whisper on the wind. . . .

"It's the Blood Prince," said the priest.

"Don't be hysterical," said old Ivan. "If you must be something, be prophetic and tell us what it means. But avoid hysteria. Please."

43

"I can't be prophetic," said Father Dimitri. "Let old Baba Yaga interpret the signs."

"If you can't be prophetic, then be quiet," grumbled Ivan. "And if I hear another word about the Blood Prince, I'll strangle you."

"It sounds like someone sweeping the train tracks with an iron broom," said Peter.

"Maybe it's Baba Yaga bringing the children home," said the priest.

The three men went to the platform. Something slow and heavy and still was moving out of the forest, along the southbound train tracks, toward them.

"Why, it's just the Imperial Express," said Peter, after staring a minute.

"Without lights? Without steam? Sneaking into town at this hour?" yelled Ivan. "What's the meaning of this?"

Father Dimitri suddenly lifted up his right hand and began blessing the train as it coasted, at inchworm speed, toward the loading platform. He prayed the prayers for the dead.

"It's a ghost train," said Peter. "Maybe it's carrying the souls of the dead to their destination. We shouldn't board it."

Father Dimitri wasn't listening, kept praying.

Ivan moved his eyebrows ferociously about on his forehead. "All your superstitious talk! You're a fool, Peter, like your son. Give me a hand—I want to see just what's on this train."

The train had finally come to a halt, a slow natural stopping of its own weighty accord. In the moonlight the windows shone like lake water, but no faces appeared. Old Ivan climbed up into the cabin of the steam engine. Peter followed, and then the nervous priest.

There was no one in the engine to handle the complicated apparatus. No one to stoke the furnace or read the gauges.

"Did everyone jump off this train as it rolled through the northern forests this morning?" wondered Ivan. "Where *is* everyone?"

They made their way back to the passenger cars, and there they found luggage and books, parasols and candies, blankets and boots, but no passengers.

"We should light the lamps," said Ivan. "Maybe we'd see a clue."

"What do you think, Father Dimitri?" said Peter.

The priest kept praying.

So Ivan lit the lamps at last, and then they saw the blood at last, and at last old Ivan with the two sets of eyebrows had to concede that there must be such a beast as the Blood Prince, because no other power on earth was wild enough to leap aboard a moving train and systematically eat passengers and crew, car by car.

And then Ivan and Peter leaped out of the ghost train all at once, realizing the Blood Prince might still be aboard. But the old priest, with tears streaming down his face, stood in the middle of the first passenger car and continued to moan out his prayers.

In her yard, Baba Yaga pounced on a spider and held it up in the moonlight. The rain had finally stopped, and she stood over a puddle. She said a few words to the spider, and the spider began spinning a filament.

The witch let the spider dangle by its own thread over the mud puddle, and she spit in the puddle. The mud cleared and the water shone as bright as Old Sophia's piece of broken looking glass.

Over the reflecting water Baba Yaga leaned, swinging the spider and singing a little song:

"When you dream, you dream of me.
Does that make me dream of you?
So I do, and if I do,
Will that make the dreams come true?"

The children looked at each other—the song had a familiar sound to it.

The spider descended until its eight scrabbling legs touched the surface of the puddle.

"The Firebird came to the children," said Baba Yaga in sepulchral tones. "Reveal to me now the treasure of its challenge."

Maybe it was somebody's dream that appeared in the puddle then: Baba Yaga's, or the spider's, or one of the guardian skulls'. A Firebird flared up in a dark space, a nameless, unknown space; it flapped its golden wings, threw back its splendid head. Beneath its shining feet rested a small dark wooden chest. The chest was so humble that only the Firebird's perching atop it made them pay any attention to it.

Then the vision faded. That was all.

"In that chest," said Baba Yaga, "is the only weapon that will save us from the Blood Prince. The Firebird appeared to you to lead you there."

"Where is it?" said Pasha, his first words to the witch.

"I don't know," said Baba Yaga. "Only the Firebird knows."

"We have to find the Firebird again," said Lisette forcefully. "So it can lead us there." Then she added politely, "Unless you mean to kill us for having seen the Firebird before you did."

"I saw the Firebird first and last," said Baba Yaga. "Such is my life. I saw it flying toward Miersk, but I didn't know why. Then I saw it again, and I did know why but it was too late."

"We've only seen it once," said Pasha.

"You've seen it twice," said Baba Yaga. "Once by the railroad tracks as you just told me, and a second time, here."

They stared at her.

"Don't you see?" said Baba Yaga, winding up the spider on its string and storing it in her dark hood for future services. "The Firebird can't lead you to the little chest, because the Firebird—poor brilliant thing which I must respect for its beauty and magic—the Firebird is dead. The Blood Prince ate its heart, and the body of the Firebird is the bright spindle that hangs right now in my hut."

The Village Grows Restless

"But what's in the chest?" said Lisette.

"I don't know, and the weaving magic of spiders and dreams won't say," said the old witch. "A spider goes back and forth, a thread, a thread, spinning a circular ladder that falls in on itself like a dream. A dream goes back and forth, a face, a gesture, and most of it is empty, unfilled air like the spaces of a web. Precious little information you get from either. But at the heart of each is the answer."

Pasha and Lisette studied their hands, feet, the dull puddle.

"Don't you understand me?" screamed Baba Yaga.

They were too frightened to admit their ignorance.

"She means," said one of the skulls dryly, "that this is only half the solution to the problem of the Blood Prince. The other half someone will have to dream."

"When I want your help," began the old woman, and she befouled the clearing with several minutes of the worst cursing heard outside a tavern brawl. Lisette was too young to understand what most of the cursing meant, but Pasha understood a little and he turned pink as borscht.

When Baba Yaga was finished, she turned, sputtering and spitting, and said, "I'll need to spend tomorrow preparing potions and poisons we might be relying on. You can start off for Miersk without me if you want. But now that you know the Blood Prince is no rumor, you might be foolish to go wandering off without protection."

The children took the witch's advice, thinking they'd be safer all together. So they spent the next day in the drying mud of the yard in which the house of Baba Yaga stood. All day long shrieks and crashes and curses sounded through the open windows as the witch worked on her spells. The skulls kept flinching on their poles.

"Our skins have been saved," said Pasha. "She must be feeling kindly toward us since she found the dead Firebird. But any minute she could have a change of heart and mash us to pulp with her iron teeth. We'd better watch our step."

"If she's not a friend, she's an enemy," said one of the skulls, grinning painfully. "I'm proof of that."

"Who are you?" said Pasha.

"That's better left unsaid," said the skull. "Baba Yaga is human and so can be loyal as well as vindictive. But I have no heart, so it's best not to trust me. I'll get you in trouble, and enjoy it too."

Pasha blanched.

"I'm sorry about that, but you might as well know," said the skull. "Don't depend on this old dry head for anything."

To pass the time, they told each other stories. Pasha told the tired tales of his grandfather's famous gallantry (they were the only tales he knew well enough to tell aloud—they were the only tales ever allowed inside his house). Lisette could think of only one story, which Pasha already knew—well, everybody in Russia knew the story of Vasilissa the Beautiful!—but to be kind, he listened to it again as if he'd never heard it.

"Vasilissa was only eight years old when her mother died," said Lisette.

Lisette's thinking of her own mother, thought Pasha.

"Just before she died, her mother gave her a magic doll. Her mother said if bad things happen to you, Vasilissa, the doll will help you, and all will be well. Then she died. Vasilissa's father remarried, a terrible woman who had two daughters of her own. This stepmother was fierce and mean. To get rid of Vasilissa, she sent her to Baba Yaga's hut for a light, thinking that Baba Yaga would eat the poor girl. The old witch gave the girl three tasks that would have been impossible but for the magic doll, who helped her every time. Baba Yaga was satisfied and gave fair Vasilissa a skull with light in its eyes—"

"Yes indeedy," said one of the skulls, listening to Lisette's story.

"—and when she returned, the light from the skull's eyes burned up the wicked stepmother and the stepsisters. And Vasilissa grew up and married someone kind and handsome."

"That's a nice story," said Pasha politely.

"But her mother was still dead," said Lisette sadly.

50

"Vasilissa had the magic doll, but her mother was still dead."

"Well," said Pasha, "that's how things are."

"Telling stories about Baba Yaga in her own yard!" teased one of the skulls. "Wouldn't she like to hear about this?"

"Oh, close your lipless mouth, you," said Pasha, and he gave Lisette a hug.

⁂

When it had been proven that the Blood Prince was no longer on the Imperial Express, the men of Miersk retired for the evening, deciding not to decide anything until the morning. As Old Sophia, the only woman who had come out to investigate, reminded them with some unusual softness in her voice, the morning, my dears, is wiser than the night.

So after the cows had been put to graze and the bread to rise and the laundry to air in the weakening early-autumn sunshine and the logs carted to the station—carted there out of habit; the train was obviously not going anywhere—the humble people of Miersk gathered around the ghost train.

Old Sophia, Father Dimitri, Ivan and Peter and Quiet Onya. Moody Grishka and his little laughing Vanya. Tanya, Olga, Marla, Bara, and Sweet Amelya, and their husbands and children. A couple of stray sniffing dogs. In short, all the villagers stood a small distance from the elegant train, a bit afraid of what to do now.

Old Ivan with the two sets of eyebrows climbed onto the railway platform. He was the oldest man in the village, a leader by disposition and by common agreement. What he said next was later agreed to be the second-finest moment of leadership in his career. (The absolute finest moment came a bit later.)

"Credit me with foolishness," he said in a voice like an earthquake. "Chastise me for my idiocy. Condemn me for the blindness that has brought sorrow to all of us."

It was not like old sour Ivan to beg forgiveness. The villagers resisted the urge to condemn, chastise, and credit him with foolishness; they kept silent, and in a minute Ivan went on.

"I have held that the Blood Prince was an idle threat, an imaginary fear suggested to us by our old wives and timid children."

"Huh!" said Old Sophia loudly—she was the oldest wife among them.

"Huh!" echoed little Vanya.

"I've encouraged the village to resist preparing for a siege by the loathsome wolf," said Ivan remorsefully, his eyebrows crushing down heavily on his lashes, his gaze cast down at the unpainted floorboards of the platform. "And yet even the children have risen to the task, departing to seek Baba Yaga to ask her advice about a threat I claimed was nonsense."

Quiet Onya blessed herself.

"That's my little Lisette, my poor child," said Grishka loudly, though everyone knew it already.

"And it's also Pasha, the son of my son Peter," said Ivan. "For all these lives I claim responsibility. You must revoke my status as an elder of this village."

Old Sophia gestured at someone to help her up, and she climbed onto the platform next to Ivan. "I am the first one to chastise you as you request," she said, and she slapped him, hard. Then she kissed him on the other cheek—to the murmuring surprise of the respectable villagers of Miersk—and she said, "Now can we stop talking about *you* for five minutes at least and decide what we're going to do?"

Ivan, admirably, took all this in stride, and he said, "Well, then, I'll tell you what we have to do. Listen."

The villagers quieted down and leaned forward.

"We have to abandon our village of Miersk, for once, for all," claimed Ivan.

The villagers instantly forgot to be quiet.

The children had found it difficult to sleep in Baba Yaga's hut because the blazing body of the Firebird couldn't be extinguished for the night like a candle or an oil lamp. The morning that Baba Yaga announced that she was ready for the return trip, Pasha and Lisette, yawning and sleepy-eyed, stumbled around the yard collecting the skulls in a cauldron and pulling up the stakes that the skulls had rested on. Baba Yaga had decided she didn't want to leave them behind, so the children put them into the house.

"Look sharp, move your heels, or do you want me to implant sets of biting teeth in the ground at your feet?" called Baba Yaga in a mild voice from the door of her hut. But despite her threats the witch seemed in a good mood. "Oh, there's no end to the fun a simple soul can have if she's possessed of a clever mind," she said blithely to the skulls in the cauldron before crashing a heavy iron lid down upon them.

Pasha and Lisette had discussed how exciting it would

be to ride in Baba Yaga's house as it wobbled on its chicken legs through the pines and birches of the dark forest. "It will be like riding in a boat," Pasha predicted, and Lisette said, "And the bushes and berries and vines will be like the green sea rushing beneath us, and the big green trees will be like dark thunderclouds around us."

But when Baba Yaga cried out suddenly, "Now we're ready! Little house, to Miersk!" the children were outside washing in a small stream nearby, and they had to run to keep up. Old Baba Yaga had no intention of letting them ride inside.

Fortunately, chicken legs, even large ones, are not the most intelligent of legs, and the house jostled into trees, pitched about wildly on the tops of slopes, and one time even fell over on its side. The children had no trouble keeping up.

"Can you imagine what they'll say when we finally show up?" said Pasha to Lisette. "Can you imagine the look on the face of that old crow, my grandfather?"

"I can imagine the look on the face of my baby brother, Vanya," said Lisette. "Imagining it is giving me the strength I will need to face my father—who will be so angry that I have gone off that he'll probably kill me when I return. I won't live to enjoy our homecoming."

"I'll protect you," said Pasha gallantly—well, it was a time for gallantry. They were going home!

❧❧❧

It was Ivan's idea that the villagers of Miersk should leave their village forever, by way of the Imperial Express.

"So poor Leo Maryushka is dead and gone, and the engineers and the boiler men," said Ivan. "You all know that years ago, when they first began laying down the tracks for this run, I pestered the workmen with questions, and I climbed aboard the first engine to come through Miersk, and I learned every bit of machinery on this iron monster. I could teach everyone else what to do in the space of one afternoon. We can leave tomorrow."

The shrieking and the scolding drove up against this suggestion like a sudden squall. Ivan covered his ears against the noise.

"It's our only home, what else do we have, where do we go, how do we survive?" protested the women. To be fair, some of the men in the village voiced their doubts, too, but the women voiced them louder.

"It's all we have, these clumsy leaning shacks. The winds needle through the knotholes and the rain always finds a seam in the roof boards to slip between, but even so we have nothing else—our little village is ours and we won't leave it!" Old Sophia called her protests the loudest.

"You want to be eaten? Like poor Leo Maryushka? Like Pasha and Lisette, like all the passengers of the train?" answered old Ivan. "You stay here in this fleabag of a village, and your own little houses will still be here but there'll be no inhabitants."

"It's stealing. We can't steal a train," said Father Dimitri.

"I won't leave the village until I'm sure Pasha and Lisette are dead," said Quiet Onya. "What if they come back and find Miersk deserted?"

"We've got to," roared Ivan, stamping up and down on the railway platform, shaking his fist. "Besides, there's no one left alive on the train to know that we're taking it! Who could mind?"

"Hit him again, Sophia," cried out Sweet Amelya. "Knock his teeth down his throat, so we don't have to listen to this heartless idea!"

Who knows what might have happened then, as the villagers began taking sides, pulling hair, calling insults, weeping with rage. Perhaps a full-scale battle would have erupted on the railway platform, and all the villagers would have killed each other, saving the Blood Prince any trouble. But a sound from down the tracks made the villagers pause in their squabbles—

And their heated blood cooled instantly, in the Arctic-cold fear accompanying the realization that it was the little house of Baba Yaga that was strutting so ominously toward them along the railroad tracks, its legs lifting straight out in front of itself like a little boy proud of a new pair of leggings. The old witch was leering wickedly from the front window. The arguing died away.

Then Quiet Onya wrenched free of her husband's arm and ran madly toward the witch's house, because she'd caught sight of the two tired figures straggling along behind, and one of them was her beloved Pasha.

The rejoicing lasted fifteen minutes. Then Grishka boxed his little Lisette on the ears, to upbraid her for leaving the village without permission, and Pasha was sent to collect gentle Milkface from the field. Four

people went into the elegant mahogany-paneled re-
served-for-very-special-travelers carriage. Readying
for a conference, they settled themselves comfortably
on the velvet maroon upholstery, eyeing with some
appreciation the handsome brass appointments, the
carpets, the little pillows in embroidered white slip-
cases left around for easing the travel-weary bones of
the wealthy.

The delegates to this convention: old scowling Ivan,
old equally scowling Sophia (though endowed with
fewer eyebrows, thus less menacing to look at), stut-
tering Father Dimitri.

The fourth member of the congregation had not
been invited to join. But as she picked at the spaces
between her iron teeth with a long jagged nail she'd
pulled from the ceiling, no one could find the right
words to ask her to wait on the platform like everyone
else.

"So talk," said Baba Yaga.

"At issue is the question—" began Father Dimitri
bravely, and the witch said, "I said talk, I didn't say
recite a speech."

The three villagers, having had little to do with
Baba Yaga personally, were nonetheless aware of her
reputation and knew there was no sense sweet-talking
her.

Ivan said, "I'm proposing we take the train and
leave the village of Miersk for good. The Blood Prince
is on the prowl and may even now be near at hand.
There's no time to waste."

"Did the children tell you they saw the Firebird?"
asked Old Sophia.

"I saw the Firebird myself," said Baba Yaga, spitting on the carpet (a little black hole burned clear through the carpet and the floorboards to the tracks below). "The children forgot to try to grab the Firebird's feathers because they are young and selfless; no omen there. But their coming to me in their youth and selflessness was an omen; and that the Firebird appeared to them, of all the children in this part of the world, that was an omen too. So you look around in this world, so you see omens at every step. There was a prophecy. I saw in a puddle a vision of a box that the Firebird thought very highly of. In that box lies the tool for triumphing over the Blood Prince. But someone will have to dream how to find it. Otherwise the Blood Prince will catch up with Miersk and destroy it."

"Why should we be tormented?" cried Father Dimitri, despite himself.

Baba Yaga rose. Her black clothes wafted around her like the smudgy arms of a fir tree seen on a moonless night. Her smell was awful.

"He wants something here that is as pure as the first snow?" she said, making a face. "Maybe that? Who knows? If he has to destroy the whole town for it, he will; that much I'm sure of. His hunger is unequaled."

"What do we have that's pure?" scoffed Old Sophia. "With our greasy clothes and our mean little ways, nothing, nothing at all."

"The Firebird pointed out something," said Baba Yaga, dangerously still.

"What does he want?" said old Ivan tiredly. Head in hands.

"He wants the dreams of children," said the witch. "Maybe?"

⋘⋙

Out of the northern forests, once every generation or so [Baba Yaga said], *a wolf walks. His eyes are poison, flames from hell, poison stars. His teeth can bite through steel. He is so evil that ordinary wolf packs scatter like chipmunks when he passes.*

There is nothing real about him, and no one understands what is unreal about him. Four hundred years he's gone by the same name: the Blood Prince.

Why does he come south only once a generation? Some say he usually lives so far north that he freezes in ice for twenty years at a time.

Why do people forget about him from one generation to the next? Because they can't believe that anything could be so bad. They keep telling themselves that they imagined it. Then they're not ready the next time he comes. It's a new horror all over again.

Why would the wolf come to plague the forgettable little village of Miersk? Of all the miserable little villages in Russia? Because the golden Firebird appeared near Miersk, to children who didn't think to try to steal its tailfeathers, children who might be able to destroy the wolf for once and for all.

But why did the Firebird appear to them, to Pasha and Lisette, of all the children in Russia? It is a question that no one can answer.

Nevertheless: Pasha and Lisette. Two weak, disobedient, ordinary children. Two friends. It is on them both that the fate of the village depends.

Or so it seems. Why else the omens?

Now: What are we going to do about it?

59

"We?" said Old Sophia.

"Yes, *we*," said Baba Yaga. "What are we going to do about it? We're all in this together. Like it or not. I'm feeling vengeful because the old hairy beast ripped the heart out of the Firebird. Besides, mean as I am, I don't want to be left all alone in the forest if the old foul mouth is roaming around." She pulled her black babushka around the edges of her chin. "A woman living all alone might be bothered a bit."

"First thing is to get away from here," said Ivan. "We can worry about finding that box later."

"I agree," said Baba Yaga.

"On the train," said Ivan.

"Why not?" said Baba Yaga.

"It's our *village*; we can't leave Miersk," cried Old Sophia recklessly. She thought, incidentally, that this might be her last sentence ever.

But Baba Yaga—almost sisterly in her calm—merely said to Old Sophia, "If you can't leave the village but you *have* to leave the village, then leave the village, but take the village with you."

"We can't *steal* a *train*," complained Father Dimitri.

"I don't know what you mean," said Old Sophia to Baba Yaga.

"Take the village with us!" exclaimed Ivan, smiling for the first time in weeks. "Why not? *Why not?*"

Pasha was nearly out of breath when he reached the field where the few cows were led every day to graze and to think things over. He pushed aside the gate and walked out into the meadow, his heart pounding, his hair every which way.

A small bit of fog had gathered like dust along the edges of the field, and the cows stood in a line in the fog, nose to tail, as if single file exploring a bit of boggy ground. Their legs were shrouded but their solid bodies showed dense and dark, like a series of boulders pushed into line.

He walked from one cow to the next, and when Milkface raised her homely head and sniffed him up and down, and regarded him for a long silent moment, and then left her place in line to begin the trek home, Pasha was more pleased than he could say. She hadn't forgotten him. It was all right.

Oh, it had been wonderful to be hugged by his warm mother, and to be kissed by his proud father, and to have staunchly endured the double-arched wordless astonishment of his grandfather, but in between all of this there was a lot that was wrong, and different, and upsetting. Why was the train sitting without passengers or attendants? Why were the villagers crowded around it in the middle of the day?

So to have the unmysterious cow swaying its slow weight along the common road, to smell her old regular cowy smell, was to feel at last that things were still normal. Life hadn't been turned upside down yet, not if gentle Milkface could still remember him, sway so touchingly next to him.

He sang to her, the song of Lisette's dead mother.

"When I dream, I dream of you.
Does that make you dream of me?

61

Dreamers holding hands are we,
Dreaming things that soon will be."

Maybe she didn't like the singing. Milkface began walking faster, picking up her hoofs and setting them down again in the hard dirt of the road, sounding like pieces of wood knocking together: *clop, clop, clop, clop*; and then faster still: *clop clop, clop clop, clop clop*.

Clop clop clop, clop clop clop. Pasha was running to keep up.

The heavy beast plowed like a thundercloud along the road, raising dust and scattering fog, her white face held aloft in some sort of anxious watching. Pasha tried to call out to her, *Milkface, stop! I won't sing if you don't like it!* But he couldn't squeeze out the words.

She had never run before. She was usually too bored to run.

She was frightened. Milkface was scared out of her cow's wits.

When they both rounded the curve that took them into the ramshackle such-as-it-was center of Miersk, they were running so hard that they couldn't stop. Pasha ran right into his father and knocked him to the ground. Milkface ran madly, headfirst, into the fourth car on the tracks, splintering the wood and splashing glass fragments all over.

☙❧☙❧☙

Nobody seemed to mind that Milkface singleheadedly had destroyed a whole wall of one coach of the train.

In fact, as Pasha regained his breath, he noticed with some surprise that the villagers of Miersk seemed to have gone crazy.

Old Ivan and sour Grishka were taking an ax to the fancy ceilings of the first passenger car. Sweet Amelya and Old Sophia were ripping out the velvet curtains of the second car. Bara, Tanya, Marla, Olga, and accompanying husbands were carefully removing the valuable glass windows from the third car. Milkface had taken care of the fourth car. Father Dimitri and Baba Yaga—an unlikely couple—were ripping the handsome siding off the fifth car. Quiet Onya was collecting the lovely little white pillows. Lisette and little Vanya and the other children from the village were rooting through the luggage of the deceased passengers, they called to Pasha, looking for rubles and jewels, guns and books: anything worth keeping.

And even the house of Baba Yaga was standing on one leg and kicking in the windows of the sixth car with its other leg.

"There wasn't any wolf chasing you," said Peter, holding his son. "It was your imagination."

"Milkface doesn't *have* an imagination," said Pasha when he could speak. "I tell you, it must have been a wolf. But what's all this commotion?"

"It was Baba Yaga's idea," said Peter. "We can't leave our village, so we're taking our village with us. We're going to rebuild the houses of Miersk on the flatbed foundations of these railroad carriages, and then we're going to start up the engine and leave this place, bringing the village of Miersk with us."

Pasha went to see what Lisette thought of all this wildness.

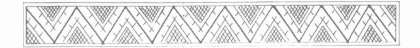

Trying to Dream the Dream

The people of Miersk, hard workers all, had *never* worked so hard as this before.

Every day they dismantled a hut, and carried the rough-hewn logs and the supporting timbers and roof beams to the side of the tracks, and then rebuilt the hut again on the platforms of the old train coaches. They carried the furniture, tin basins, clothing, icons for the holy corner, the great precious stoves, the occasional samovar, the ropes and knobs and buttons that get collected during a life in a hut. They found things that had been lost for years.

Every night they slept with determination. Each person wanted to be the one who would dream the dream that would tell them where the magic chest was and how to open it. They tried so hard to dream the dream that some of them became insomniacs. Some only got headaches in their sleep. Some dreamed about trying to dream the dream, with no luck.

Every morning before the building began again, Baba Yaga held a session on the railway platform to

64

hear everyone's dreams, to try to tell if any dream was *the* dream.

Old Ivan dreamed the same thing every night: that he was the Tsar of Russia and lived in a silver palace in Moscow. After a while Baba Yaga stopped asking him his dreams, because they were all the same.

Father Dimitri dreamed of floating up to the sky in ecstasy before God. Baba Yaga rolled her eyes at that.

A couple of the men and a couple of the women were embarrassed to say their dreams in public, so Baba Yaga made them come, one at a time, into the engine cabin and whisper their dreams privately to her. Villagers outside could hear her screaming with laughter at a number of these dreams.

Quiet Onya dreamed that Pasha and Lisette were still lost. Waking up was a miracle come true, she said.

Old Sophia said she was too old to have dreams.

Pasha wanted to be the one, oh, so hard! Every morning when he woke up, he tried not to roll over on his mat, not to think what day it was, not to figure out by the sounds of people moving below who was up and who was still abed. Instead, he tried to keep any dreams from rushing away from him, fast as a train at top speed heading for unspeculable land-scapes. He tried to catch one small insignificant sen-sation from the dream still lingering in a side room of his mind, and then to gently coax back as much of the dream as he could get. At the point when he wasn't sure if he was remembering anymore or imagining new things instead, he opened his eyes and snapped the dream into place in his head, chained it there for good by the sight of the *real* roof slanting above his head, the smell of the *real* morning meal teasing him to get up.

If he dreamed the dream, oh blessed fortune! Maybe the old scowling mask of his grandfather's face would look down on him with something sweeter than annoyance.

Day after day Baba Yaga listened to Pasha's dreams carefully. They were always involved and storylike, and the other villagers grew to anticipate them with interest. But day after day the old witch would shake her head and say, "Lively enough, but just not *right*. Not the answer." Seeing his downcast expression one day, she added, "Not yet, anyway."

Lisette's dreams were wry dancing things, usually about her mother. Sometimes little Vanya and her father Grishka were in them too, but her dead mother was the main character. Every night in Lisette's dream her mother sang to her:

> *"When I dream, I dream of you.*
> *Does that make you dream of me?*
> *Dreamers holding hands are we,*
> *Dreaming things that soon will be."*

"That doesn't help," said Baba Yaga every day. Grishka always looked down at his feet when it was Lisette's turn to tell her dream. The gruff-spoken man had never realized his daughter missed her mother so much. As much, maybe, as he did.

Where was the wolf while all this was going on?

Well, nobody knew.

If indeed it had been the Blood Prince, out of sight on the road, who had scared old Milkface into a top-speed gallop, then the wolf was around and watching their activity. But why didn't he attack? Any night of the week he could have stolen into the village and, hut by hut, ended their lives. It wasn't Baba Yaga's spells that were keeping him away; her spells weren't strong enough to have any effect on *him*. Not a chance.

Old Sophia had an idea. "Maybe *he* doesn't know where the magic box is. Maybe he's waiting for one of us to have the dream, so he can race there ahead of us and make off with it forever."

Everyone agreed this was a likely possibility.

Still, people were careful not to walk alone, even in the middle of the day, even in the center of the village.

And at night most people slept closer to each other than they used to, as they tried to dream the dream.

It was an unbelievable evening when Pasha had to climb up the ladder to his loft, and curl up in the hay and blankets, and he was in his house and out of it too, because that day the villagers had taken the planking off the roof of the hut, getting ready to rebuild the hut the next day on the foundation of a railroad carriage. The house was as open to the night sky as a cow pen or a pigsty might be. The whispering winds in the forest kept up a ceaseless conversation with the trees all night long. If it starts to rain, Pasha thought, I could go downstairs and crawl under the table.

He awoke in the middle of the night and heard a noise. He leaned over the edge of the loft and saw his mother. The moonlight was so bright that she hadn't needed to light a lamp. She was rolling dough for pies. Pasha knew she rolled dough in the middle of the night to calm her nerves. She was always hearing wolves howling and baying in the forest, and her blood turned to liquid fire in her veins at the sound.

Pasha climbed noiselessly down the ladder and dipped a ladle into the water jug and took a drink. Neither Quiet Onya nor Pasha spoke, because Ivan and Peter were both asleep, but Quiet Onya gave Pasha a hug before he climbed back up the ladder to sleep again.

✺✺✺✺✺

Finally the day arrived.

Finally!

The village of Miersk had been completely wrenched up off the ground and had been nailed to the flatbeds of the railroad carriages. The only things left to mark the old site of the village were the churchyard with its leaning stones and the paths which now knotted a broad empty field. The paths were like the lines of a spiderweb, and the empty spaces in between the lines were the worn sites of huts, the tired earth where people had lived.

It was sad to look at, surely. Sad to think about leaving the churchyard behind, where the relatives of the Miersk villagers were in their final rest.

But the Imperial Express had been transformed as if by magic into the village of Miersk.

A handsome job, all agreed: a village like none other on earth.

First was the bold engine, and then the coal tender;

68

then followed a couple of log huts, each with some nice carved detail on the eaves or around the windows, painted in bright colors. Then, its small spire lifting religiously toward heaven, the small chapel and the hut of Father Dimitri. Then some more huts, and three flat carriages with fences built around them: one for the cows, one for the goats and ducks, and one for the sheep. Then a carriage loaded high with coal to fuel the train through the first part of its journey.

The final carriage was the first-class carriage from the Imperial Express, preserved intact so it could serve as a meeting place for all the villagers. Why shouldn't they enjoy the fancy velvet upholstery and the brass fittings?

Off the end of the first-class carriage swayed the sign that had always hung on the railway platform to tell the passengers on the train what village they'd stopped at. The sign read

MIERSK

and everyone was thrilled at the idea that it would swing back and forth as the village rolled along.

"With as little commotion as possible, let's get this village moving," said Baba Yaga. "No prayers, Father Dimitri, please; no speeches, Ivan; no weeping, Quiet Onya. Gather your children and take your pies off the windowsills and we'll be off."

"This is a sight to see," observed one of the skulls. (Baba Yaga had driven a pole with a skull on it into the roofs of several huts, so the skulls could yell out if they saw the wolf approaching.) Now, however, the old witch was feeling less than conversational, and she gave the skull a look so fierce its blood would have been frozen if it had had any. The skull fell silent.

"We can't leave yet." It was Grishka at the door of his hut. "I can't find Lisette."

"That'll be her fault. We're going," ordered Baba Yaga.

"I see her," called one of the skulls. "Over there in the graveyard."

Lisette was at her mother's grave, leaving a bouquet of wildflowers, trying to say good-bye without knowing how. "We'll come back someday, Mama," she whispered, "or I will alone, I promise. And I'm sure Pasha will dream the dream so your little Vanya and Papa and everyone else will be saved from the wolf."

"Lisette!" yelled her father.

"Lisette!" yelled all the skulls, mocking.

The engine gave out a great black flower of smoke that hung in the air above the long, wheeled village; the whistle gave out a whistle that slid through the morning stillness with the sharpness of a needle; the villagers gave out shrieks of terror and delight as their huts began to shiver and jostle and fidget a bit on their moving foundations.

"Lisette!" yelled Grishka.

She came running from the churchyard, across the spaces where the huts of Miersk had stood just ten days before; and her father held out his hands, and Lisette gave a mighty leap, and the silly skulls all cheered when, at the last possible second, she boarded the village.

☙❧☙❧☙❧

Suppose there were a traveler or two camped on the little promontory above the lake south of Miersk. It would be a good place to camp, of all the places in that wolf-infested woods: high enough to see for quite a ways, shielded from the wind by a stand of gnarled pines. And along the far edge of the lake ran the railroad tracks. Travelers camping there would be too far away to hail the passing train, but they could watch the train from a distance, see its twin in the reflection of the water.

If anyone had been camped on the promontory that morning, what a view of the village they'd have been treated to!

Coming across the trestle bridge at the end of the lake that funneled into a small river, pompous, odd, bright, toylike from the distance: the village. First the muscular black engine, emitting its black smoke in a long festive curling canopy. Then (But how can this be? the travelers would ask themselves) a set of huts on wheels! Huts with steeply pitched roofs, and odd maroon drapes flying from the windows; huts with children riding on roofs; huts linked by massive connecting chains and bolts; ropes strung between the huts, with wash hung out to dry in the wind. And a chapel—how could there be a chapel on a train? but its gold-painted cross was visible for quite a ways—and some pens with, oh, it looked like cows! geese! ducks! sheep! And then a mound of coal, and then a first-class carriage, nearly forgettable compared to the carriages that it followed humbly.

The travelers would turn to each other, high on the far hill, and ask each other what could be odder than that, a caravan of huts, an ordered movable village? And if they kept watching, they'd see a hundred yards behind the first-class carriage, strutting along full of purpose, the high-stepping house of Baba Yaga, with the old witch herself evident at the windowsill, staring this way and that!

Oh, thought Pasha from his place on the roof of his house, this is fine and handsome, if only there were travelers up on that hill across the lake. How smart a picture we would look, rolling along like the most natural thing in the world, a village on wheels.

～～～～～

In their first day's travel they came upon no other railway station, no switch engineer, no juncture of lines.

"Well, we're traveling slowly," said Peter, who was learning to handle the engine from the stern teaching of Ivan. "With such an odd assortment of buildings dragging along behind us, we have to move slowly or we might jostle our homes to crumbs and dust. Besides, Baba Yaga's house would have a hard time keeping up if we went too fast."

"Teach me to drive the engine," begged Pasha.

"Absolutely not," said Ivan.

"Oh, please, please," said Pasha, *"please?"*

"You're not strong enough. You're not even tall enough," said Ivan.

"Am I *anything* enough?" said Pasha sullenly.

"You're young enough to be beaten for being willful," said Ivan. "Now go tell Grishka we're getting low on water."

"Oh, I'm so luckless," said Pasha. He went to find Grishka.

"Tell them to stop at the first stream we come to, and we'll camp for the night," said Grishka.

So as the sun slid down behind some clouds, an edge of it showing red as a geranium, the village came to a halt for its first night. The villagers tramped down the banks of the stream with buckets, to get water for their evening meal, for the train. Sweet Amelya picked some flowers and tried to stick them in the mouths of the guardian skulls, but the skulls kept spitting them out and telling her not to bother them.

Pasha ran back to the cow pen and poked his face through the poles of the fence. "Milkface, over here! How do you like being a traveling cow? Do you want to be milked now?" His old friend leaned down her awesome face and licked Pasha's forehead. She didn't seem to be minding the ride at all.

Baba Yaga's house came walking up alongside the village. "Well, there's some small distance we've put between ourselves and the Blood Prince today," called the witch proudly from her window. "How did everyone's houses fare? Everything survive the journey?"

A chorus of voices answered her: My old aunt's soup bowl broke, a window cracked, the hens laid eggs in the clothes basket but they rolled around and smashed. But nobody's voice was too upset; everyone seemed to be enjoying the chance to have some excitement.

Quiet Onya opened her window and let the current brood of Clucks and Clacks go out to scratch the soil for their dinner. The hens, seeing the great legs of Baba Yaga's hut, threw themselves devotedly at the heavenly hennish vision. The hut backed away with a sidestepping embarrassment, but the hens pursued it with mindless chattering attachment. Quiet Onya and Peter and Ivan and Pasha had to gather Cluck and Clack and their relatives and force them back into their hut.

For the nighttime Grishka and Lisette took some stakes and drove them into the soil fifty yards down the line past the engine, and fifty yards up the line past the first-class carriage. On the stakes they placed the skulls, whose glowing yellow eyes would shine out as a warning signal in case a freight train might be wanting to use the tracks that Miersk was camped on. No collisions if they could help it.

After the various families had eaten their evening meals, they gathered in the first-class carriage to talk things over. Little Vanya had great fun opening and slamming the individual doors to all the private compartments until Lisette gathered him up in her arms and told him to stop.

Father Dimitri was talking. He told them that Baba Yaga had told him that they would have to dream the dream soon, before the winter snows came; how could they find a chest if the world was blanketed white, hiding all its secrets?

"So I know it's exciting, to be charging away from the wolf at this speed, at last," he said, "but try to dream the dream tonight. Clear your minds of worries and cares, court fancy, entertain yourselves. We have to dream up the answer soon."

Then Old Sophia told a story about the Firebird,

and Peter told a story about Vasilissa the Beautiful and her magic doll, and Sweet Amelya did a dance that lasted far longer than anyone's interest in it, and Lisette sang her mother's song, and at last they all went off to their own huts to do the hard work of dreaming.

❧❧❧

"Well?" said Baba Yaga the next morning.

"I didn't dream anything," said Peter. "I was so tired I fell asleep like a piece of stone and no dreams came to me."

"I dreamed I was the Tsar of all the Russias," said old Ivan, "and I made all the rules of the land, and was served my meals on plates of gold—"

"You old fool, let someone else speak," said the witch. "Your dreams are as familiar to us as the morning light, but hardly as helpful." Old Ivan sat down, tucking his hands in his sleeves, testily stomping his boots on the carpeted floor of the first-class carriage.

"I dreamed of a pack of turtles," said Old Sophia. "That's what we're like, isn't it? Carrying our homes about with us like this?"

"No good, no good, we need a *dream*," screamed the witch. "We haven't got all year! Do you know the body of the Firebird in my hut is losing its brilliance, little by little? A bad sign! My spider spins a web over my eyes every night when I sleep, a bad sign! This is not a holiday! Pasha, my dear boy, tell me what you dreamed, at once!"

"I dreamed there was a high trestle bridge," said Pasha nervously.

75

"Was it the trestle bridge that we crossed yesterday morning? What about it? Something underneath it? On the other side? What?"

Little Vanya suddenly squirmed off Lisette's lap and slammed the door to the compartment. Lisette knew why he liked the sound: The door fit so precisely into its jamb, and the tongue of the lock slid so neatly into the doorframe, with such a satisfying metallic click. It was efficient and handsome, that door, unlike the crude, ill-fitting wooden doors of their huts, which one had to tug and scrape to open or close, and to tie with rope to keep fast: a tedious business.

But Lisette also knew that Baba Yaga was in her worst humor in the mornings, when she was listening to everyone's dreams, and it didn't do to upset her. So she grabbed for her little brother. Vanya let out a volley of excited nonsense syllables meant to express in no uncertain terms that *he wanted to slam the door. Now.* Lisette said, "Shhh, shhh, shhh."

"Keep that little beast silent or you'll be sorry," said Baba Yaga. "Pasha, answer me: Which bridge? What about it? Where was the box?"

"I don't know. I didn't see," said Pasha unhappily. "It was a small dream."

Vanya escaped Lisette and slammed the door again, and crowed with delight.

"You've all got to work harder!" yelled Baba Yaga. When she was angry she smelled worse, as if something inside her clothes was scorching them. Lisette grabbed her baby brother again and slapped his palms.

"I dreamed an odd thing," said Quiet Onya. "I dreamed that there wasn't enough food to feed my babies. I had a dozen babies." She looked embarrassed. "So maybe I'll bake some bread and leave it at the side of the tracks in case there are any hungry travelers in the vicinity."

"I dreamed of someone singing my mother's song again," said Lisette. "Someone bright like the candles in the chapel.

'When I dream, I dream of you—' "

"We all know the song by now—excuse us from it, please," snorted the witch. "Sweet Amelya?"

"I dreamed I was a star in the heavens," said Sweet Amelya, getting up, "and I did a little dance that went something like this . . ."

"Sit down. Stop that," said Baba Yaga, and Vanya punctuated her order with another slam.

In frustration the witch turned to the little boy, and her eyes widened as if she would make a spell. But as she did, Father Dimitri came in the room, having just finished his morning prayers, and he put his hand on the boy's head in a greeting and a blessing, and the witch couldn't curse a child so recently blessed, so she rushed from the room with a little scream and refused to speak with anyone for the rest of the day.

❧❧❧❧

By the end of the second day of traveling some of the glamor had already disappeared. The village hadn't passed through any other villages yet; there'd been nothing but the endless forest stretching out on either side of the rails like a sea. An occasional stream, sometimes a cliff, sometimes a bridge. Pasha got tired of looking ahead for a trestle bridge. Maybe his dreams were just ordinary dreams, maybe there was no answer to their plight to be found within his humble nighttime visions.

"If we could go faster," Pasha complained to Milk-face, as he milked her that evening, "maybe we would *get* somewhere. But with that old house on its chicken legs hobbling behind us, we have to drag along at a snail's pace."

The friendly cow munched away at her dinner without comment.

"And for all we know, the Blood Prince is still following us," said Pasha. "Who can sleep at all, knowing that it may be just a matter of time till our paths cross?"

Milkface bobbed her head sympathetically.

"I want to be the one who has the dream," said Pasha. "Nobody pays attention to me. My old grandfather is as miserable as a viper; he never told me he was glad to see me back when I returned with Baba Yaga. He never apologized to me for calling me a liar when I told him I'd seen the Firebird."

The cow swayed her head back and forth as if to say, Well, what can you expect from a man with two sets of eyebrows?

"Well, sure, he's the leader of the village, I *know* that," said Pasha, "but can't a leader pay some attention to his own grandson? Treat him as if he's more than just a silly boy?"

The cow stopped chewing for a minute, turned her head back to look at Pasha.

"Oh, I know *you* love me," said the boy, "but it would be nice if he did too."

The cow considered this, then continued her dinner. Pasha sighed. From the first-class carriage behind him he could hear the happy slamming of doors. Little Vanya was having a fine old time all by himself in there.

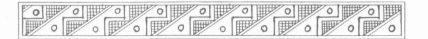

The Secret of the Box

After ten days of travel, after ten days of useless dreams that only made Baba Yaga more and more furious, Old Sophia looked at herself in her reflecting glass and sternly said to herself, "Do something to raise Baba Yaga's spirits or she'll get so disgusted with us that she'll abandon us. And like it or not, we need her. For protection—if not for company."

So one evening, when the men had gone off to look for water for the cooking of suppers, and the village was at a standstill on a lonely embankment of gravel, Old Sophia lit the fire under her samovar and invited the women of Miersk to come to her hut for the reading of tea leaves.

Pasha and Lisette and little Vanya were playing a game of hiding and finding. Pasha hid in the cow pen, between Milkface and one of her obliging companions; Lisette found him. Then Lisette hid in a woodbin built onto the back of the chapel; Pasha found her. Vanya hid in the same spot every time his turn came around: in one of the compartments in the first-class carriage, behind one of the wonderfully slammable doors. He screamed with laughter every time he was found, and he never wanted to give the other two a chance to hide.

Inside Old Sophia's house the tea was poured, one glass at a time. Around the table sat Quiet Onya, Bara, Marla, Olga, Sweet Amelya, Tanya, and Baba Yaga, who was pretending to be uninterested but who was actually fascinated. (She'd never learned to read tea leaves; it was generally considered too domestic a manner of prophecy for a woman of her tastes and talents.)

Old Sophia peered at the pattern of leaves left at the bottom of the glass of Quiet Onya, and she said, "An intricate pattern, an interesting pattern. . . . Your joys and sorrows come bound together tightly, Quiet Onya—I can scarcely tell one from the other. Might you open a home for weary travelers one day? You might, I think you might. Either that or . . ." But then she shook up the leaves quickly.

"Me next," begged Sweet Amelya, smiling sweetly.

"Your dancing feet will lead you near to someone with a rich purse and a nice big beard," said Old Sophia, "but take care, Sweet Amelya. Don't step on his toes. Never step on his toes!"

"The guessing of children, this!" said Baba Yaga suddenly, throwing her tea out the window. "Tea leaves are about as accurate as—as . . ." She fished about in the sleeve of her cloak. "As the dreams you lazy villagers have been having. Useless. I'll show you some real fortune-telling. Old Sophia, spill some water on the table."

"There's no water to be had," said Old Sophia, insulted, although in fact there was plenty of water. After she'd planned this whole evening as an entertainment. Baba Yaga taking over as usual. There was no gratitude in that woman, none.

"Then some tea, anything to reflect the light." Baba Yaga had found her spider, and was coaxing a filament out of it.

"I wouldn't waste my good tea," said Old Sophia.

"Oh, go on, Old Sophia, spill some tea," urged Bara, Marla, and Tanya. Old Sophia shook her head. Sweet Amelya reached for the triangular piece of mirror and set it down on the tabletop, saying, "Will this do in place of water?"

"We'll see, we'll see," said Baba Yaga, climbing on top of the table. She began letting the spider down.

Everyone leaned forward. Even Old Sophia, cursing herself for her interest.

The spider's legs touched the glass. A murky film condensed below the surface of the glass, and an image began to form. Everyone could see it—far more exciting than tea leaves!—but no one could name it at first. Not for a minute, not for two minutes; but in the third minute Baba Yaga saw what it was, and called it out at the same time that all the skulls posted outside the huts let out a unanimous yell of warning—

"The Blood Prince!"

❧❧❧❧❧

The men, struggling up the embankment, heard the skulls cry out, and they dropped their buckets of water and ran as if flames were at their feet.

Pasha, searching for Lisette, was on his hands and

82

knees under the hut where Father Dimitri was living. He froze, knowing that the skulls would never lie about this.

Lisette was standing on the roof of the first-class carriage, near the very end of it. She'd planned to climb down the rungs nailed onto the end of the carriage after she'd watched Pasha searching all the rooms for her, and then run off to hide in one of the places he'd already searched. She froze where she was, too, a terrible fear touching all the sides of her throat with dread.

From the windows of Old Sophia's hut peered the women of the village, Baba Yaga pushing the others out of the way.

It was Peter who reached the top of the embankment first, and looked ahead of the engine and saw the awful sight.

Forty feet up the line, having wandered away from the game, little Vanya was squatted down in the gravel to the right of the tracks, scraping in the stones with an old wooden spoon and singing to himself.

A hundred yards away from Vanya, on the other side of the tracks, leaning forward out of a screen of berried bushes, eyes ferocious in their intensity, was the Blood Prince. Horrible as could be imagined, and true as true.

"Watch out! Beware! Teeth of doom, jaws of doom, gullet of doom," chanted the skulls in a sort of hysterical chorus.

The Blood Prince set his eyes on the little boy and began inching forward.

Baba Yaga had finally burst from Old Sophia's house,

and she saw what was about to happen. The spider still dangled from her right hand. Her magic helpless against the Blood Prince, she could only scream to divert the wolf: an awful, paralyzing sound. It had no effect. The wolf kept on.

"It was *Vanya* who was having the dreams!" screamed the witch aloud. "VANYA!"

But it was Peter who ran forward, pulled himself into the cab of the engine, set the train going with a sudden, jerky motion, hoping to cut off the wolf's access to the little boy by pulling the train between them.

Peter didn't know that his son, Pasha, was underneath the train, nor that Lisette was standing, petrified, on the end of the roof of the first-class carriage.

⸎⸎⸎⸎⸎

When the train moved forward, a number of things happened.

The Blood Prince took no notice of the train at first, and just kept stalking toward little Vanya. But after a minute the train slid along the tracks between the wolf and the small child, and then the Blood Prince lifted its snout and sniffed the air with a low back-of-the-throat growling that sounded like underground caverns collapsing.

Baba Yaga advanced furiously on the wolf, her spider still dangling from her fingers like a toy on a string. She knew the wolf could leap on her and consume her in a few bites, but she was so angry at the wolf's threatening Vanya that she wasn't thinking just now about being eaten. Her hair bristled away from her head like flames from a comet.

84

Not stopping to watch the confrontation, Old Sophia threw herself out the door of her house and scuttled around to the other side of the tracks. Now she was near enough; now the wolf was hidden from sight by the train. She scooped up Vanya as if he were a mound of washing and turned back to the door of her house. Vanya shrieked at the rough handling, and Old Sophia paid him no mind.

When the train had started forward, Pasha had thought that his last minute on earth had arrived. He had no time to dart out from under the wheeled huts, so he dropped face first in the dirt and drew in his breath to make himself as thin as possible, hoping that none of the carriages was so low-slung that it would take a slice off his behind or off the top of his head.

But he heard the village rolling above him—somewhat giddily he found himself thinking that many persons had crossed a village but had anyone before this ever had a village cross *him*?—and finally he felt the last car drawn over him. It felt like someone pulling off a heavyweight mechanical blanket; it felt wonderful. It felt wonderful not to be dead. He stood up. Looked down the tracks. Saw the shadowy heap that he suddenly knew must be Lisette—and he realized that she must have been hiding up on top, and been thrown from the roof of the first-class carriage when the train started abruptly. And now she was revealed, forced out of hiding.

But no one else knew what had happened to Lisette because they were all watching Baba Yaga and the Blood Prince approach each other—and then they watched old Ivan hurry out to meet them both, scowling all his eyebrows fiercer than ever.

꿏꿏꿏

Everyone saw what happened next except Lisette, who appeared to be dead.

The Blood Prince and Baba Yaga and old Ivan came within nine feet of each other, each one equally distant from the other two.

Ivan and Baba Yaga stared at the Blood Prince with eyes so wide and fierce that it seemed they might never close again.

But, terribly, the Blood Prince opened its mouth and drooled—what came out of its mouth was red as roses. And then its tongue moved, and the two others realized that it was speaking.

"I want the child's dream," it said.

Ivan (bless his soul) got up the courage to say, "What you want isn't for giving or for taking. It can't be done."

"You hellish demon, dreams aren't trinkets," said Baba Yaga, whose spider had finally realized what was going on and was trying to crawl into the witch's sleeve.

"You don't imagine you'll survive, do you?" said the Blood Prince. "I want the child's dream."

"*We* don't even know it; he doesn't talk yet," said Baba Yaga. "Now be gone, you old terror; there's supper to get."

"You can have my dream," said Ivan.

"Don't bargain with him!" shouted Baba Yaga, but it was too late. The Blood Prince, as near as it could be seen, smiled.

"Don't you know," said the wolf, "that only a child

with a dead mother can dream this dream? But I'll take your generous offer anyway. Are you ready to go?"

"He's a fool, wolf; you don't want him or his dream," screamed the witch, but Ivan made the Sign of the Cross, turned white, and said, "I'll keep my word. I'm like that. Known for it my whole life through. I'm ready."

"You have to bargain, old poison eyes," yelled the witch. "What's your payment for the old man?"

"No payment at all," said the wolf, "and you know it, hag. He volunteered his dream." It turned to Ivan. "It'll be no good to me, your dream, but I'll take it— for the fun of it. But just for sport, because it's how things are done, I'll offer to leave you your life if you can answer three questions. . . ."

Baba Yaga saw that all was lost. Pompous old Ivan, brave fool, poor thing, had talked himself into his own death. And for nothing: The wolf didn't even *want* his dream. She backed away from the two of them, and then turned and ran back to the train tracks as fast as her old legs could carry her. "Let out the throttle and wave good-bye to your father," she shouted at Peter. "The faster we get out of here, the better."

❧❧❧❧

The skulls were screaming, "Don't forget Lisette! She's all in a heap on the tracks!" So while the villagers ran to their huts and the train began moving forward, Grishka leaped and raced to the place where Lisette had fallen.

Pasha was crying, "Is she dead, is she dead?" and Grishka didn't say anything, just picked up his daugh-

87

ter and ran back to the train. Pasha followed, wishing now that the train had killed him, too.

His mother, Quiet Onya, was standing in the door of their hut. She reached down and pulled Pasha up into the moving doorway. "Turn around and get a last look at your grandfather," she said through her tears. "Old Ivan has sacrificed himself for us."

The train was moving faster. Pasha didn't even have time to stand up: He just rolled around on his stomach and stared out the open door. It was his first glimpse of the Blood Prince—face to face with his old mean grandfather, gone white as a ghost, getting smaller by the second. Pasha leaned out the doorsill and was sick.

Old Ivan heard the train picking up speed and prayed that someday the village would be safe. He knew he'd made a terrible mistake, and his death would be no help at all . . . but if they could get away, a little bit, outdistance the wolf for a while, maybe Baba Yaga could figure out how to discover what kind of dreams little Vanya had. . . . Maybe his sacrifice would give them a little time, at least.

"First I'll take your dream," said the Blood Prince, and Ivan felt his knees give out, unlatch like broken hinges. He fell on his hands and knees and the wolf came right up close, two feet, one foot, five inches now. . . . The wolf opened its mouth and out came the tongue, which went across old Ivan's forehead left to right, burning like a fiery rag. Then it withdrew.

Ivan thought: What is it I feel now?

He couldn't think of how he felt.

"Now for the questions," said the wolf. "If you can answer them correctly, you can keep your life. If not, well, that's no care of mine."

Ivan supposed it would be better to answer the questions with right answers rather than wrong ones, but he couldn't remember why.

The last of the train disappeared around the bend as the wolf said, "What was the name of Lisette and Vanya's mother?"

An easy question. Ivan considered how to phrase the answer. "Grishka called her Lissa to her face. But by everyone else she was fondly referred to as Vasilissa the Beautiful. After the old tale. An affectionate nickname, because she was fair and kind and lovely to see."

"You know the story of Vasilissa, and I do too," said the wolf. "Everyone in Russia knows of Vasilissa and her magic doll. It was first given her by her mother before the old woman died. And Vasilissa was to give it to her daughter, Lisette."

If Ivan had been feeling things as he should, he would have felt astonishment. Vasilissa and her magic doll was a famous story that everyone in all the Russias knew! When the villagers had called Lissa the name of Vasilissa the Beautiful, they'd been speaking kindly, flatteringly. Not accurately. It couldn't be.

"Where is the magic doll?" asked the wolf. Its second question.

Old Ivan didn't know. He was sure little Lisette had no dolls; Grishka had become so fierce in recent years that playthings were not allowed in his house. But

Ivan remembered what Baba Yaga had said about her original prophecy and he took a chance. He said, "It's inside a box, safe and sound."

Life or death now with the wolf's third question: "Where is the box?"

Ivan didn't know! He didn't know! That's what everyone had been trying to dream, but nobody knew yet!

So he opened his mouth to say the last words of his life, and just as he did a shooting star crossed the night sky and made him make up an answer: "In between the day and night, in between the wrong and right, in between the dark and light, it's in between— in between."

And the answer may not have been specific enough for the wolf, but neither was it incorrect, because the wolf's eyes opened with anger. But its word was its word. "You cheat!" it growled.

Behind old Ivan, on the train tracks, Baba Yaga's hut on its chicken legs was trying to tiptoe past, trying to catch up with the village. It had been wandering by itself and had missed the train's hasty departure. Ivan turned and ran to it. "Little house, let down your front face and let me come in." And it did and he was inside it safe and sound and the fading glow of the body of the dead Firebird lit up his face that had no expression on it. And the wolf disappeared into the forest.

The spirits of the Miersk travelers were lower that night than they'd ever been.

Old Sophia, who knew more about health and sickness than anyone else, said that Lisette wasn't dead. But try as they might, the villagers couldn't wake her up. Father Dimitri said prayers: no use. Baba Yaga anointed her with special oils whose origin she wouldn't disclose: no use. Grishka held up little Vanya so the boy's plump rosy face was next to his sister's pale one: no use.

In vain Baba Yaga tried to pry out of little Vanya whatever dreams he might have been having. "The child's dream," the Blood Prince had said. But Vanya would not learn to talk all in one evening, and Baba Yaga could not lift his scalp off with a spell and look inside his head. (Grishka wouldn't allow it.)

In another hut, Quiet Onya and Peter and Pasha sat in the darkness, trying to think of what life would be like without old cranky Ivan as head of the family. Peter wept for his father, and Pasha wept for his grandfather and for Lisette, and Quiet Onya shed quiet tears for Ivan and Lisette, and everyone else who had ever been sick or lost, and the cat, Mousetrap, tried to comfort them all.

"This is a hopeless venture," said Quiet Onya.

"We are a luckless lot," said Peter.

"Poor Lisette," said Pasha.

Things went on like this for quite a while, until Pasha began to be bored with crying. So, promising he wouldn't wander away, he went outside to be with Milkface.

"Is Lisette going to die, Milkface?" asked Pasha, rubbing his nose in her warm forehead. "Tell me what you think."

The cow thought about things for a while, then

lifted her head and watched a bright star stream across the sky.

"So many people dead already because of this," said Pasha. "Leo Maryushka, and now my old grandfather, and maybe Lisette—"

Milkface turned her head so one eye could stare back at Pasha. Then she tilted her head as if listening for something special, and she mooed.

"Are you talking about the shooting stars?" asked Pasha. The sky was quite crowded with them tonight.

But there was a sound, a scratching, a moving through the grasses at the side of the train, and then almost before Pasha had a chance to be afraid, there appeared the walking hut of Baba Yaga, which, with all the commotion, hadn't even been missed yet.

"Oh, it's high time you returned!" said Pasha loudly, feeling like scolding.

"What? Is that my boy?" came a familiar voice, and Pasha leaped up to see if it could be true.

꙰꙰꙰

Well, they were glad to have him back, they were glad he'd survived, but old Ivan was a different man now.

He behaved as an old man should, kissing Peter and Quiet Onya and Pasha, scratching the head of Mousetrap, telling them the story of his interview with the Blood Prince, but something was missing from him: his crankiness, his bravado, his bossy snarls, and his sulking silences. There seemed to be no real expression in his face.

"The Blood Prince took his dream—that must explain it," Peter told Old Sophia when she came to see

92

Ivan. "He used to dream he was the Tsar of all the Russias. Now when he sleeps he has no dreams."

"And when he wakes he has no character; this is bad," said Old Sophia. "But the dream isn't the only thing the Blood Prince took from Ivan."

"What?" said Quiet Onya.

"Haven't you noticed?" said Old Sophia. "The Blood Prince also took away his second set of eyebrows."

They hadn't noticed it, but it was true. When the wolf had licked Ivan's forehead, it must have burned one set of eyebrows right off.

"Maybe things will yet right themselves," said Old Sophia, looking at the sleeping old man. "We know more now than we did before. We know that Grishka's wife was really and truly Vasilissa the Beautiful, and that what we need to find is the magic doll. Why the doll is a danger to the Blood Prince I don't know. But try to sleep well. We'll think on all these things in the morning. The morning, you know, is wiser than the night."

Oh, but what a night to be wiser than!

Only old Ivan and poor Lisette got any sleep that night, for the sky was peppered with brilliants, littered with diamonds. Stars rolled back and forth in the deep blue, plentiful as snowflakes, swift as raindrops. No one could sleep for the light or the noise—"I know they're not making any noise," said Sweet Amelya, "but I *feel* as if they are." The villagers climbed up on the steep slanting roofs of their huts and put their arms behind their heads to watch the unearthly display, and the skulls told funny stories to each other and wouldn't keep quiet even when asked.

When the morning sun sent its first ray lancing out over the horizon, Lisette and Ivan woke up and all the villagers fell asleep.

"Baba Yaga," yelled Lisette, shaking the old witch, "wake up! Wake up! I've had the dream!"

"They won't wake up. None of them. Even the cows are dozing," said Ivan.

"Pasha! Vanya! Father!" shouted Lisette, but they slept as if they'd sipped a sleeping potion.

"They'll sleep until they're ready to awaken, I'll wager," said Ivan.

"But I had the dream," said Lisette. "I know where the box is!"

"Oh, do you?" said the old man.

"Don't you want to hear my dream?"

"I suppose so."

Lisette looked at him. Something was odd about old Ivan. But she told him the dream anyway.

"I dreamed my mother came to me in a boat hitched to the moon. But she herself was brighter than the moon—her face was almost fiery as it looked at me. There were stars whirling about as if they were tied to the ends of strings, making circles in the air. She got out of the boat and sang me her song:

'When I dream, I dream of you.
Does that make you dream of me?
Dreamers holding hands are we,
Dreaming things that soon will be.'

94

But this time there was a second verse:

> *'In between the day and night,*
> *In between the wrong and right,*
> *In between the dark and light,*
> *The buried box is shining bright.' "*

"But that doesn't say *where* the box is buried," said Ivan.

"No," said Lisette, "but my mother opened up her arms and spread them wide, as if to indicate the spot. And do you know where she was standing?"

"No, I don't," said Ivan.

"She was *standing*," Lisette was shouting with excitement, "she was *standing* in the *center* of our own old *village* of *Miersk!*"

Before Their Very Eyes

Turning the village around wasn't easy.

It was three more days before they reached a railroad yard where the carriages could be turned around on a turntable. And what an entrance they made into the railroad yard at Bovgorod! Engineers and assistants, laborers and townspeople, officials and peasants stood side by side, gaping, as the ramshackle village trundled through the city.

Of course the yard captain recognized the engine as belonging to the old Imperial Express, and was all for clapping chains on the villagers for their grand theft. But Peter calmly told him that the Blood Prince was following them, and the quicker they reversed their direction, the less chance there'd be of the Blood Prince's arrival in Bovgorod.

And as the yard captain was hesitating, the hut of Baba Yaga walked into the railroad yard, the old witch at its window, picking her iron teeth defiantly with a scimitar.

"Turn the village around!" ordered the yard captain.

"It will take all day to explain to the authorities what we're doing," said the yard captain, "but you'll be free to go by tonight."

So Pasha and Lisette went off to explore the city.

"Let's see the churches," said Lisette.

"The grand homes. The big stores!" said Pasha.

Bovgorod buildings grew around them large as trees, dense as cliffs, ornate as icons. People hurried by, speaking languages that sounded like nonsense. A man with a balalaika winked at them and sang them a song about "love that can cross the widest sea." And everywhere, pigeons.

"It's like bunches of huts piled atop one another," said Lisette.

"It's like a dozen plays all going on at the same time," said Pasha.

It was a day for forgetting about the Blood Prince. So many people to look at! The city was so crowded with people, it seemed hard to imagine anyone being anyplace else.

Pasha and Lisette bought a roll in a shop and ate it while walking along the canal. This was their first chance to spend time together since Lisette had woken up from her dream, because Grishka had been so relieved that Lisette hadn't died that he hadn't let her out of his sight; he couldn't bear to. But today was special, and Grishka was busy at the railroad yard helping to turn the train around.

Lisette finished her half of the roll and said, "I'm

sorry for dreaming the dream, Pasha."

Pasha continued to chew his half.

"I know you wanted to dream it," she said. "I didn't mean to."

"You couldn't help it," he said.

"Even so," she said, "I always thought your dreams were better than mine."

"So did I," he said.

"Well, there it is," she said.

They walked across an elegant bridge with fancy wrought-iron lamps.

"It was a brave thing for Ivan to do, to challenge the wolf," said Pasha, "and if *I'd* had the dream that night, he never would have cared or noticed, because after that night he wasn't the same. So it's all right that you had the dream. Truly it is."

"It was my mother's fault," said Lisette. "She didn't have to come to me like that."

"Oh, don't *cry*," said Pasha.

They leaned over the balustrade of the bridge, shoulders touching, and watched the cold river steal in silent sheets away from them.

The children were staring through the window of a building in the center of town, astonished, hungry, delighted. There was a roomful of tables with white cloths spread over them, and sparkling china and crystal glasses, and many people were coming in and going out, sitting to eat in groups of two and four and six and twelve. The trays of food that were being carried elegantly around! The fancy dresses of the ladies! (Pasha said the ladies looked as if they were all wrapped up in the curtains and drapes of the Tsar's palace: velvet and silk, fur and lace, golden cords and silver tassels.) The men were proud and smiling (though, Lisette thought, perhaps a bit cleaner than men really needed to be. Cleaner than any of the men from Miersk, that was for certain). If they could be invited into this odd building, what a difficult time it would be to choose what to eat! Bowls of clear soup with lemon slices floating in them; cuts of meat steaming under floods of gravy. And when a man wheeled a cart by with an arrangement of pastries, Pasha and Lisette nearly screamed their approval. The pastries were as elaborately constructed and pleasingly designed as many of the buildings they'd seen in the city! Swirls of cream topping, loops of colored frosting, full-bloomed roses on tiny cakes, pagodas of meringue bolstered with colorful banks of raspberries, blueberries, odd berries they didn't know . . .

As they turned to leave, deciding that their whole adventure had been worth it for this most unbelievable vision, a voice called out to them from the door of the building, a voice that knew their names. They turned, and running toward them, whole and sound and neat as a soldier: the wide-eyed conductor, Leo Maryushka!

Not eaten by the Blood Prince at all!

The children found themselves hugging him as warmly as if he'd been their own father, tugging on his sleeves with their urgent questions: "How did you survive? We thought that the wolf—"

Leo Maryushka chartered a droshky and bundled the children inside. They were so excited to be getting a ride that they could hardly listen to his story. But Leo Maryushka told them that he had gone to the authorities in Bovgorod as Quiet Onya had asked him, and he had begged for the help of the Tsar's men in seeking Pasha and Lisette. The authorities had found his request astoundingly bold and impertinent, and they had clapped him in chains for several weeks, just to teach him not to be so forthright. So the day that the Blood Prince had leaped aboard the Imperial Express, Leo Maryushka hadn't been there. He'd been in the jailhouse, under lock and key.

Pasha and Lisette told Leo Maryushka about the transformation of the train from the Imperial Express to the village-of-Miersk-on-wheels. The conductor made a face at the thought of that beautiful train being scrapped in favor of huts and pens, but when the droshky deposited them all in the train yard, Leo ran forward and greeted the engine with a shout of joy.

The yard captain was as delighted to see that Leo Maryushka was a friend of the villagers of Miersk, and he immediately suggested that Leo make the return voyage to Miersk with the villagers—"To keep an eye on the engine, which, after all, is the property of the Tsar."

But Leo Maryushka didn't like Baba Yaga. "She shouldn't be involved in all this," he muttered to Peter and Grishka. "Who's to say she isn't in league with the old wolf? Better to be parted from her company, my friends, that's my advice."

"She's stood by us firm and true," said Peter, "and no one has come to harm by her yet, Leo."

Leo said, "I've traveled a good distance on the Russian rails, Peter, and found some people opposed to trains. Away to the south, they've called the train the Devil's Wagon. Not a sentiment of mine! As you know! But a train that is accompanied by its own Baba Yaga— oh, an incredible Witch's Wagon it is, and I don't like it."

"Things are not always as they seem," said Peter patiently. "Trust us, Leo; we've grown to trust her."

Leo grunted an indeterminate answer to that; but he was not in the graces of the authorities, and he was reluctant to displease them by refusing a voyage on the Witch's Wagon—which was what he called the train from then on. He was in the train yard with a packet of extra clothing, therefore, when the train was ready to leave.

By nightfall the train had been turned around and set on the opposite track, and the yard captain made a short speech; he wished them well on their journey, and if no word ever came of them it would be assumed they'd all been eaten by the wolf. If, on the other hand, they somehow succeeded in thwarting the wolf for once and for all, well, then congratulations all around! Good-bye now.

And the citizens of Bovgorod waved out a wild farewell; the man who played the balalaika rushed up to the door of Grishka's hut and thrust a rose into Lisette's hand—and then when the cow pen passed, he rushed up and gave a rose to Pasha too. Milkface began a gracious mooing and the other cows took it up; the skulls cheered. And following the caboose,

Baba Yaga's hut performed a fetching little dance step. The applause was very satisfying.

Up to now they hadn't traveled at night, afraid of collisions; but the yard captain had assured them that due to fears of the Blood Prince there were no trains using that line, and that they could travel without worry. So for the first time, Lisette had a chance to sleep in her own little cot while the village was in motion.

It was nicer than she'd been able to imagine. The hut swung back and forth, left and right and back again, and it seemed like falling asleep in a tree. Little Vanya, in his trundle bed near the stove, cooed in his sleep, having his baby dreams—

Did he dream the same things that she did? Had he been dreaming of his mother all along, singing her song and opening her arms to the village of Miersk? There was no way of knowing.

Of course Lisette was nervous, terribly nervous, in a way. What if her dream hadn't been the right one? What if it had been an ordinary dream that was leading them all in the wrong direction? What if the Blood Prince was even now lying in wait for them back at the site of the old village? What if the dream was a trap?

There was only one consolation.

When Baba Yaga had heard about old Ivan answering the questions of the Blood Prince—and when she'd realized that Lisette's mother had indeed been Vasilissa the Beautiful—she said, "Now I know that your dream is the true one. Now I know why he's been after this village, of all the villages in Russia.

Why the Firebird came to Miersk, of all the places to visit. Don't worry, even in death Vasilissa won't let ill come to us."

Then Baba Yaga looked through her strange eyes at Lisette and said, "I knew there was a reason I didn't eat you and Pasha when you came to my hut. You must have recalled your mother to me."

For four days they traveled under the sun and moon both, stopping only to take on water or timber or to give the cows a chance to amble on the grass a bit. The cold weather was coming; frost on the windows, ice on the ponds. Everyone bundled up in layers and layers, beginning to think that maybe everything would come out for the good, and they could resettle their huts where they belonged: on good strong earth.

But when there was only one day's journey left, the skulls let out a scream that caused Peter to grind the village to a halt as quickly as the brakes would take hold. The engine stopped twenty feet from the edge of the trestle bridge that crossed the river. The bridge was in flames. "I see a wolf on the other side," called out one of the skulls. Yes, yes, the Blood Prince had caused the bridge to burn to keep the village from crossing.

Ivan, Grishka, Peter, Father Dimitri, Leo Maryushka, and Baba Yaga looked glumly at the deep ravine. Its sides were too steep to scale, and the river running through it too deep to ford; and though the distance from side to side wasn't enormous, it was too far to jump.

"I could fly over in my mortar," said Baba Yaga,

"but it doesn't take riders. It won't go for anyone but me."

"We can leave the village here," said Peter, "and come back and build another bridge later, when there's time. But for now we've got to get across. The wolf is looking for that box too. It's certain that we should find it first."

"Rope. I'll make a rope walkway. I'll fly it across," said Baba Yaga.

"I wouldn't trust a rope walkway made by a witch," mumbled Leo.

"Don't," warned Peter, "Leo. Don't."

"You what?" said Baba Yaga to Leo Maryushka.

Leo stood his ground. "How do we know you're not just leading us back into the jaws of the Blood Prince?"

Baba Yaga smiled. A little too widely. "I'm not doing the leading. We're following Lisette's dream."

Leo said, "You could have told her mind what to dream. The Blood Prince could be waiting for us back in Miersk."

Baba Yaga said, "Of course that's where the Blood Prince is—we just saw him over on that side. Is this the thanks I get, Peter? Grishka? For escorting this miserable train through the thousand-year forests? To be accused of treachery and malice? Is this a suitable payment for my efforts?"

"He doesn't know you," said Peter, wishing Ivan were around to set things straight. Ivan was there, of course, but only in body. Peter took in a deep breath and did the best he could. "Allow him his uncertainty,

Baba Yaga. He spent all that time in jail for the sake of Pasha and Lisette."

"I know your strength," said Leo, as the villagers began drawing around. "I know your power, Baba Yaga. But how do I know you won't cause a rope walkway to tumble into the ravine when we're halfway across? Get rid of us for once and for all?"

"I have no need to get rid of anyone but the Blood Prince!" said the witch. "I could have caused a dozen derailments if I'd wanted to hurt the stupid people of Miersk. I could cause you to have a sudden disconcerting inability to breathe," she said to Leo, "right now, if I chose."

Pasha had elbowed his way to the front of the crowd, and he said, "When the walkway is done, I'll cross it first. That will prove that it's safe."

"Ropes! Now!" cried the witch, and villagers went running to gather up all the spare coils of rope available. "And I'll hang you with them when the walkway has served its purpose," muttered the witch, glaring at Leo Maryushka.

Climbing into her mortar, Baba Yaga took hold of one end of the village-long stretch of rope, and she flew across the ravine four times, looping the rope around two trees, one on either side. Villagers took planks from the sides of the first-class carriage and laid down an uneven flooring across the double ropes. And Pasha, who had once been so timid of Baba Yaga, was the first one to cross, his bare heels and toes clenching anxiously to the surface of the planks. But the crossing was safe, easy.

Peter followed. Then Quiet Onya carrying Vanya; Grishka leading Lisette. Next the other women of the town, hitching up their skirts delicately; then their husbands, pretending not to mind the great drop beneath them. Everyone, in fact, until only Leo and Father Dimitri and Baba Yaga were left.

"I see I was mistaken," said Leo Maryushka, "and I apologize, Baba Yaga, for doubting you."

"Don't be so sure you were mistaken," said the witch coolly. "I could still cause the walkway to collapse while you are making your crossing."

"So you could," said Leo Maryushka. "Well. As you will, then." And he set out across the walkway.

"Don't do it, please," begged Father Dimitri in a low voice. "Mercy, Baba Yaga."

The witch merely stared at the back of the train conductor, who crossed in safety.

She turned to Father Dimitri. "My patience, if you must know, is nearly at an end," she told him. "*Very* nearly at an end."

❧❧❧❧❧

The cows, sheep, geese, ducks, and chickens were left locked up in their pens. Pasha waved at Milkface (a little wave, when no one was looking). It wouldn't be long now! Did Milkface have a homesickness in her heart like the homesickness the villagers had sometimes confessed to?

The villagers were gathered now on the other side of the ravine, leaving behind the train; a silent conductor and a furious witch stood as far apart from each other as they could get. "We're all ready: it's the last stretch of the journey," said Peter. "Let's go."

Then Baba Yaga's house tried to cross the walkway. The witch kept screaming at it to stay where it was, but it wouldn't obey, and the skulls cheered it on with a wicked glee. Several times it threatened to topple into the ravine, but finally it arrived safely on the other side and scratched its feet proudly in the pine needles.

"Don't be so self-satisfied," said Baba Yaga, rapping it on the door with her broom. "I'll burn you soon as set foot in you again if you're going to be bold."

But when the villagers began to march single file toward the desolate field of the old village, the house followed right along behind, the glow of the dead Firebird hardly visible in its windows.

"This is it, this is it," said Pasha to himself, "the end of our long journey. If we're lucky we'll find the box, and inside the box will be the doll. If Baba Yaga's vision was right, then the doll will be strong enough to defeat the Blood Prince once and for all." Then they could resettle their houses where they belonged, the Imperial Express could begin to run again on its old schedule, and everything would be back to normal—

Except for Ivan, of course.

He walked along with the other villagers, no sign of his arrogant leadership evident. A bit of mud was on his sleeve, only a subdued light behind his eyes. He stumbled over branches which a week earlier he'd have leaped over without thinking. His conversation made little sense.

Pasha found himself walking just a little behind his grandfather, and off to one side, to be able to reach out and steady his elbow should he falter.

107

Leaving the flat place in the forest that had once held the village of Miersk in its lap had been a triumphant thing; it had been a valiant escape, a successful daring escapade. Returning to the flat place in the forest where their homes had once been clustered was sobering and saddening.

"Look, it's our own old piece of sky," said Old Sophia, gesturing above her. "Even the sky doesn't look the same anyplace else."

"I thought we had our homes with us," said Grishka, "but this place is our home, too. At least it feels to me as if I'm coming home."

"No time for teary-eyed memories," said Baba Yaga. "We're close to the moment of crisis. The Blood Prince is around, just waiting for us to find that doll. Save tomorrow for moaning and groaning." She led the villagers to the graveyard. "So now, Lisette, you must tell us where the box is buried."

"There wasn't any box buried with my wife," said Grishka hurriedly. "I know that for sure."

Lisette thought back to her dream. "There wasn't any specific spot pointed to," she said. "I dreamed that my mother opened her arms up, and—it was the whole village she was pointing to."

"We can't dig up the whole village," snapped Baba Yaga.

"I can't do any better than that," said Lisette apologetically.

"Can your spider and my mirror point it out?" asked Old Sophia.

"If they could, we'd have been here two weeks ago,"

said the witch. "Only the dream or the Firebird could have told us where it was."

"Well, I'm going to start digging," said Peter. "It can't hurt."

"It could take weeks!" yelled the witch.

But the villagers paid her no attention. With sticks and the limbs of old trees they began scraping at the worn earth of their old home ground. Even the hut of Baba Yaga scratched, rather ineffectually, in the topsoil.

"This is no use!" shouted the witch. "Lisette, you use your brains!"

"Baba Yaga," said Grishka, "don't yell at my daughter again or I'll knock your iron teeth out."

The villagers paused in their excavations, expecting to see Grishka turned into a snorting pig or a pile of dead leaves. But the witch merely whirled around on her heel and went storming into her hut, slamming the door behind her so fiercely that it echoed around the clearing.

Lisette smiled inside herself so hard that she thought her face would burst from trying to keep it in.

Pasha was digging next to his grandfather near the foundation of their old hut.

"This is a hopeless job," said Pasha.

"Maybe yes, maybe no," said Ivan.

It was hard for Pasha to be with his grandfather. He wished that Ivan would suddenly stand up, take charge again, boss everyone around, order people here and there, argue with Old Sophia, and scoff at Father Dimitri, and even ignore Pasha again—that he would be himself: gargantuan, authoritarian, important. Instead of just scratching away in the dirt with a stick, no more sure of himself than Pasha was.

Pasha leaned back on his heels for a minute and thought.

His grandfather hadn't believed him when he'd announced that he and Lisette had seen the Firebird; he'd said that any fool would have tried to grab a tailfeather. Pasha would never have had the heart to pull a tailfeather from a living Firebird! But now the Firebird was dead, and after several weeks the glow from its ember-bright body was nearly faded for good. Maybe Baba Yaga would let him take a feather to give to old Ivan. Maybe somewhere deep in Ivan's changed character there was a small piece of the heart that would still appreciate it. Might still see the significance of the gift. After all this time.

"I'll be back in a minute," Pasha said to Ivan.

"If you're not here, you're somewhere else," said Ivan. "That's how things are."

Pasha smiled with some pain and got up.

At the edge of the clearing a familiar contemplative face appeared, surveying the busy villagers in the barren field of their old home, blinking her eyelids in slow satisfaction. "Milkface!" said Pasha. The cow must have broken out of the pen and followed the villagers across the makeshift bridge. And behind her, in single file, the other cows.

Milkface gave Pasha's cheek a big raspy lick and laid her heavy head on his shoulder for a minute, as if to give him a hug.

"Look, the cows, they want to come home, too,"

shouted Sweet Amelya. "They have more sense than we do."

"Graze here," said Pasha. "Things will be done soon."

Then he went up to the hut of the witch.

"Take it," said Baba Yaga. "I've about given up with Miersk. I was hoping that keeping the Firebird's warm body might cause one of us to dream about it—because the Firebird knew where the chest was buried—but nothing of the sort has happened. Take the whole body, I'm about to leave. I'll go back to the train and collect my skulls and see if I can keep out of the way of the Blood Prince."

"Why are you so sure of our failure?" asked Pasha.

"Look at that!" The witch pointed a bony finger out the window. "Two dozen foolish Russians scratching the scalp of the earth with little sticks. That chest won't be found by anything short of magic, but they're still out there as if they're planting turnips, so glad to be home that they've forgotten the wolf is around. He's in the underbrush, he's on the edge of things, you'll see. The minute they come close to the chest, he'll know it. He'll be out of the woods and at their throats, and they'll be so exhausted from days of work, they won't have the strength to fight back."

Pasha figured the witch was probably right. "But they're glad to be back. Look, and they're trying, trying hard."

"I'm through with it, I tell you."

"Well, thank you for the help anyway," said Pasha.

"Bah, thanks. I was in it to protect myself, not a gathering of idiots."

"Whatever, it was a help," said Pasha. He considered for a second: Was he brave enough now to lean forward and give the witch a kiss, for a going-away present? No, he definitely was not.

"Little house, let down your door so I may go out," he said, and the hut obligingly lowered the doorsill to the ground level, and out Pasha walked, the Firebird in his arms.

The villagers saw him, straightened up, let out a unanimous breath of wonder—Pasha, little unimportant Pasha, crossing the empty village with the dimly glowing body of a Firebird in his arms! Father Dimitri almost blessed himself. Quiet Onya glowed with pride, nearly as brightly as the dead Firebird itself. Grishka inexplicably grabbed Vanya and Lisette in his arms and clutched them tightly, his breath quickening. Baba Yaga watched from the window of her hut, Milkface from the edge of the clearing. Leo Maryushka took off his cap with the lovely gold braid. Only old Ivan, still on his hands and knees, with his back to his grandson, didn't see.

Halfway across the empty lot, right in the center of what had once been the village of Miersk, Pasha stumbled and let out a cry as if he'd been shot.

They saw Pasha fall to the ground; they saw him open his arms and thrust the Firebird's body up into the air. It hung for a second in the air above the center of the abandoned village, and everyone except Pasha and Ivan saw what happened then.

A creamy-gold tailfeather fell of its own accord out

of the Firebird's suspended body. The tailfeather flipped around in the air and dived, quill first, into the ground. The Firebird's body then crumpled in a heap off to one side.

"I'm burned, the Firebird warmed up, I'm burned," Pasha was crying into the earth.

The villagers rushed forward. Quiet Onya and Peter gathered up Pasha in their arms, and Baba Yaga came hurtling out the door of her hut, her hut itself not far behind. Leo Maryushka laid the bright feather in his cap, and then the villagers dug there in earnest.

Old Ivan marched over and felt Pasha's brow. "He'll be fine—just a shock," he said, and looked at the villagers pawing at the earth. "So it's here, is it," he said, and got to work digging.

They were all in each other's way, shoulder to shoulder and knee to knee, so afterward everyone claimed to have been the first to feel a corner of the chest. Only as large as a loaf of bread, it had been buried three feet in the ground at the center of the village of Miersk. Bound with leather straps and secured by a lock whose key was missing, the box was lifted out of the earth and set down next to the body of the Firebird. Pasha, starting to recover, joined the circle of villagers surrounding it.

The lack of a key didn't stop Baba Yaga. She carefully undid each of the leather straps, brushed the earth off the box, and reached into her sleeve for her spider. Knowing what was expected of it, the spider lowered itself on a thread from Baba Yaga's hand and made its way down the side of the box to the lock. It slipped inside the keyhole—and half a minute later the lock snapped open. The spider, impervious to praise, retired to its home in the witch's sleeve.

◦◦◦◦◦◦◦

As Baba Yaga lifted open the lid of the box, there was a thundering sound.

Was it a rumbling in the graves of the churchyard? It seemed to come from the earth, not the sky. The villagers looked around them.

There'd been no skulls on the lookout to warn them about the Blood Prince.

But the thundering noise wasn't from the racing feet of the wolf—though the wolf was bearing down upon them with a snarl like a comet tearing through the air. The wolf, wicked and swift as it was, didn't have the bodily weight to shake the earth like cannons going off at half-second intervals. The deep thundering racket—Pasha screamed when he saw it—was from the hoofs of gentle Milkface, who was charging determined as a train across the open field, aiming to intercept the wolf.

Sweet Amelya leaped up and screamed, "Mercy!" as the Blood Prince and Milkface collided some thirty yards from them.

Milkface died instantly, her heavy head thrown up into the sky like a gruesome offering, her hoofs delicately established—for a few seconds—against the chill autumn sky, looking for all the world like a cow ascending to heaven as a saint and a martyr.

The wolf wasn't killed—but it was stunned, thrown backward, knocked out of its death course. The cow's

114

blood streaming from its jaws, it rolled over on the ground, dizzy, disconcerted, stopped for a moment at least, its momentum disturbed.

With trembling hands Baba Yaga held up the box to Lisette. Lisette reached in and took out the little wooden doll that had belonged to her mother, Vasilissa the Beautiful.

How a doll with a painted mouth could speak was a thing nobody could understand, but the little matrushka said, "You found me:

> *In between the day and night: in a dream;*
> *In between the wrong and right: in a dream;*
> *In between the dark and light: in a dream.*

Your mother buried me here one night, sleepwalking, dreaming about this day. Your mother was a woman who attended mightily to her dreams. Now move aside: I must do my work."

The villagers parted and the doll danced out to meet the wolf. What a dance! Sweet Amelya was so jealous.

The wolf had arisen from the ground near Milkface's body, and it was moving slowly, uncertainly forward, growling under its breath.

"I'm as old as you are," they heard the doll cry gaily. "You don't scare me, old bristle face!"

The wolf began to whine.

"In between the day and night," cried the matrushka, "in a dream!"

The wolf stopped in its tracks.

"In between the *wrong* and *right*," cried the matrushka, "in a dream!"

115

The wolf began to back away, its tail between its legs.

"In between the DARK and LIGHT," cried the matrushka, "in a dream!"

The wolf raised its head in terror, wailing—

"Be *buried*, Blood Prince, out of sight," cried the matrushka, "in a *dream!*"

And the Blood Prince rolled itself up into a sliver of coal-black light and was extinguished out of the world before their very eyes.

The matrushka turned back to the villagers. "It was the best I could do," the doll said. "Who knows when you'll have to meet the Blood Prince in your dreams now? But never on the earth, never again, no, no."

Straight to Lisette: "I have the magic of all the ages in me. I am the cure for dark times, and I am passed on from mother to daughter. I am every girl's toy; I am every woman's memory. . . . The wolf would kill to find me and destroy me, and through the ages he has been searching. Oh, but your mother the dreamer saw this day coming, and she died of fright that the wolf would kill you to get me," said the doll. "But Firebirds soon learn that I am the cure as well as the curse. And the Firebird came to lead you back to me until the wolf intercepted again."

The doll danced around. "I am the cure as well as the curse, and the day is not yet over!"

How the villagers reestablished their village is a story that can be guessed by anyone who has heard this much already, but there are two parts more that might come as a surprise.

The first one is that when the Blood Prince disappeared out of the realm of the actual and into the realm of dream, the dream he'd stolen from old Ivan must have been squeezed out of him. The instant the Blood Prince disappeared, Ivan straightened up and said to Pasha, "Stop lazing there on the ground. You haven't been hurt—just a little shock. Get up and show some respect." Pasha stood up, his eyes filling with grateful tears. He reached for the tailfeather of the Firebird to give to his grandfather, though he suspected that now his grandfather would behave toward the gift with a belittling attitude.

Did Ivan get his second set of eyebrows back? No. Did Milkface pull herself to her feet and amble over to Pasha? No. What had been done had been done.

But no one, not even Baba Yaga, had ever witnessed what happened next.

Pasha picked the tailfeather of the Firebird out of Leo Maryushka's cap and noticed that the limp body of the Firebird was glowing a bit more brightly than it had earlier. He felt his cheeks go red, and he said, "Look," but Ivan and Baba Yaga were having an argument off to one side about how to get the Imperial Express across the ravine now that the trestle bridge was gone, and the villagers were engrossed in the discussion. "Look," said Pasha, turning pale now, as the Firebird began to stir her flaming feathers. Nobody paid attention to him but the hut of Baba Yaga, which tiptoed forward around the edge of the crowd and, seeing what it did, fell right over in amazement. "Look," said Pasha in a whisper, his face going pink again like a rose, and this time Lisette heard him, and little Vanya. The Firebird rose up in the air and spread its wings preparing for its final flight, and Vanya's face turned bright—was he recognizing something he'd seen in a dream?—and Lisette felt her heart nearly stop for joy.

For then Lisette knew that she had done all the right things, and been as brave as she'd been asked to be. Vanya was smiling as if in his baby thoughts he was equally sure. For just before it flew away forever, a streak of white fire brushed into the autumn air, the Firebird said in a voice Lisette had not yet forgotten and which little Vanya would fondly remember, "When I dream, I dream of you," and little Vanya opened his mouth to say the first word of his life, the first word that any child ever says.